# EX LIBRIS

## VINTAGE CLASSICS

# HEART OF DARKNESS

Józef Teodor Konrad Korzeniowski was born in the Ukraine on 3 December 1857. His parents were Polish and had both died in exile by the time Conrad was eleven years old. His uncle became his guardian and looked after him in Krakow until he was sixteen when he went to sea. He worked on both French and British ships before he became a British citizen in 1886 and changed his name to Joseph Conrad. In 1896 he married Jessie George and they later had two sons. His first novel, *Almayer's Folly*, was published in 1895 and he went on to write many more, as well as short stories, essays and a memoir. His most famous work, *Heart of Darkness*, was inspired by his experiences working on a steamboat in the Congo. After its publication in 1899 in *Blackwood's Magazine*, *Heart of Darkness* was first published in book form in 1902 with the story *Youth*, which also features the character of Marlow. Joseph Conrad died on 3 August 1924.

OTHER WORKS BY JOSEPH CONRAD

JOSEPH CONRAD

# Heart of Darkness

AND

Youth

WITH AN INTRODUCTION BY
Tim Butcher

**VINTAGE BOOKS**
London

Published by Vintage 2007

4 6 8 10 9 7 5 3

Introduction © Tim Butcher 2007

*Heart of Darkness* was first published as *The Heart of Darkness* in
Blackwood's Magazine in 1899
*Heart of Darkness* was first published in book form with
*Youth* and *The End of the Tether* in *Youth: A Narrative,
and Two Other Stories* in 1902

Vintage
Random House, 20 Vauxhall Bridge Road,
London SW1V 2SA

www.vintage-classics.info

Addresses for companies within The Random House Group
Limited can be found at: www.randomhouse.co.uk/offices.htm

The Random House Group Limited Reg. No. 954009

A CIP catalogue record for this book
is available from the British Library

ISBN 9780099511540

The Random House Group Limited supports The Forest
Stewardship Council (FSC), the leading international forest
certification organisation. All our titles that are printed on
Greenpeace approved FSC certified paper carry the FSC
logo. Our paper procurement policy can be found at:
www.rbooks.co.uk/environment

# CONTENTS

# INTRODUCTION

Seldom can an author have achieved his aim for a novel more completely than Joseph Conrad with *Heart of Darkness*. In an author's note written in 1917, Conrad described his hope to instil enough power in the sombre theme of the book that it would 'hang in the air and dwell on the ear after the last note had been struck'. Few could dispute that this is what he did. It was first published in 1899 as a three-part serial in the monthly *Blackwood's Magazine* and in complete form three years later, alongside *Youth* in one volume, *Youth: A Narrative; and Two Other Stories*, but, more than a hundred years on, *Heart of Darkness* still resonates. Modern film-makers and writers allude to it routinely and some of the book's contents, like 'the Inner Station', 'Mr Kurtz', 'The horror! The horror!', have become key parts of literary iconography.

Where argument begins, however, is where it has always begun, ever since Conrad struck the 'last note' in *Heart of Darkness*: the debate over what the book's sombre theme actually is. The debate is not just ongoing, it is yawning. Over a century after it was written, diametrically opposed conclusions are still being drawn about *Heart of Darkness*. Some critics view it as deeply racist, while others see it as an attack on the racism of colonialism; some critics view the book as largely psychological, while others believe it to be mostly historical; some believe it is a critique of the corrupting power of wilderness, while others believe it a parable of humanity's weakness no matter what its setting.

In terms of narrative structure, *Youth* is very similar to *Heart of Darkness*. Conrad's seafaring narrator, Charlie Marlow, appears first in *Youth*, telling an assembly of four unnamed characters – another narrator, a lawyer, an accountant and a director of companies – a story from his time away at sea, and a near identical frame is used in *Heart of Darkness*. But between the first book and the second, there is a quantum leap in scope, ambition and sophistication. In literary terms *Youth* is an adolescent while *Heart of Darkness* is a fully formed adult.

Both stories were based on Conrad's own experiences as a

merchant sailor and it is hard to overestimate the role and influence of his maritime career. He was no junior deckhand who spent a few months as crew on a clipper round Cape Horn for the thrill of it. Conrad spent twenty years at sea between the ages of 16 and 36, and saw much more of the world than was normal for people in the late nineteenth century. The sea was his *alma mater* and he worked hard not just as crew member but at his studies, learning English (his mother tongue was Polish and he spoke French, Russian and German before tackling English) to a sufficiently high level that he could qualify as a Master Mariner in the British merchant navy, a significant seafaring achievement. Conrad is remembered as an accomplished writer who was also a mariner. His old shipmates might remember him better as an accomplished mariner who was also a writer.

His two decades as a sailor provided the seam of experience from which he mined his early fiction. In *Youth*, a novel that deals with the young's perception of their own invincibility, Marlow describes a journey that ended in disaster with his boat catching fire and sinking off the East Indies, forcing the 20-year-old to put to sea in an open boat. It is a dramatic story of bravery and determination but this exact same thing happened to Conrad early in his career at sea.

Today a survival story like that would be turned instantaneously into newspaper features and film scripts but Conrad lived in a more thoughtful age. It churned in his mind for years before finally emerging as a novel, not as a swashbuckling story but as an observation on the untrammelled optimism of the young. In his 1917 author's note, he wrote: '*Youth* is a feat of memory. It is a record of experience; but that experience, in its facts, in its inwardness and in its outward colouring, begins and ends in myself.'

Even more profoundly dramatic were Conrad's experiences in the Congo where his seafaring skills gave him personal exposure to one of the most dark and secretive projects of the nineteenth century: the staking of the Congo River basin as the private property of Leopold II, King of the Belgians. It is important to remember that when the Congo Free State was founded in 1885 it was not a colony in the traditional sense of the word, claimed by an entire European nation. Instead the million square miles of rainforest, savannah, swamp and waterway were staked by a single man, King Leopold, the largest private estate in history.

But it was not just an exercise in vanity on an unimaginable scale. It also involved unfathomable cruelty. Publicly, the founding of the Congo Free State was presented as an act of enlightenment, of taming wilderness and bringing civilisation, Christianity and commerce to a place of primitive savagery. In reality, much darker forces were at work, as the king's colonial agents set tribe against tribe in pursuit of plunder; first ivory, later raw rubber.

Under King Leopold's aegis the first genocide of the modern era was committed. Millions of Congolese were slaughtered to generate revenue for the king across the water. They died in the ethnic cleansing and battles of frontier wars fought between Leopold's agents and Arab slavers who had been in the eastern Congo much longer than white outsiders and were not happy to be usurped. But once the Arab slavers had been defeated, Congolese tribes were persecuted brutally *pour encourager les autres*. Colonial agents invented a uniquely vile if apparently counter-intuitive way of making Congolese villagers increase their production of goods – the agents would have the hands of prisoners hacked off to show what happens to the disobedient. The best estimate is that between three and ten million Congolese were killed in just over two decades starting in 1885.

What made the project all the more sinister was the way it was hidden from the outside world. Private companies in Belgium acted as fronts for King Leopold, carefully selecting those who would be employed in the Congo Free State and ensuring its true nature stayed hidden. Any European explorer or adventurer who ventured into the Congo Free State without signing up as an employee of one of these companies was hounded out, persecuted, even murdered. And throughout, the illusion of a civilising act of philanthropy was maintained to the outside world.

For a short time Conrad became personally involved in this sinister project. He did not just witness what was going on in the Congo, he became part of the whole colonial exercise. This made him complicit with one of the greatest ever crimes against humanity and Conrad's inevitable feelings of personal guilt must be considered when trying to understand how *Heart of Darkness* came to be written. Conrad's involvement only lasted a few months but he became, essentially, a hired hand of King Leopold. It was in the early days of the Congo Free State when the king's agents were crying out for people who knew about boats. The equatorial rainforest that covered much of the territory was almost impenetrable and it made good practical sense to make use of Africa's mightiest waterway, the Congo River, and its web of tributaries that covered an area the size of the Indian subcontinent.

In 1890 Conrad passed an interview in Belgium with representatives of the Société Anonyme pour le Commerce du Haut-Congo and was then hired to go to the Congo to work on the river's longest navigable reach, the thousand-mile section between what would later become Kinshasa, the city at the top of the rapids that guard the mouth of the Congo River, and Kisangani, the port city built as far up river as you can travel by boat before cataracts once again make the river impassable. Privately, Conrad wrote that childhood curiosity was one of his main reasons for going to the Congo. The western half of central Africa was one of the last parts of the continent to be penetrated by white outsiders and the region around the headwaters of the Congo River was, in his words, 'the blankest of blank spaces on the earth's figured surface'. But what he found when he got there was that the opening up process had cast the region not into light but into darkness.

The six months he spent in the Congo Free State left him scarred, both physically and mentally. To reach the bottom of the navigable stretch in 1890, there was no option other than to trek through two hundred miles of disease-ridden, parched mountain savannah to circumnavigate the cataracts on the lower river. In the diary he kept on his five-week-long yomp, he described how his group wandered listlessly along a trail marked by the bodies of dead natives, white officials routinely beat natives with staves and his European companion, Prosper Harou, was reduced within days to a pale, febrile wreck vomiting bile in a hammock borne by native bearers. When he reached the settlement built where Kinshasa stands today he found a tiny stockade, primitive, disorganised and staffed by colonial agents of dubious morals.

The river journey was even more wretched for Conrad. The

skipper of his boat fell sick and Conrad had to take over, nursing the tiny steamboat each of the thousand miles upstream until finally reaching his company's outpost at the foot of the falls. The company agent there, Antoine Klein, was ill and Conrad tried to save him by taking him back downriver, but the agent died en route. By the time Conrad got back to the lower settlement, he too was so ill he barely made it out of the Congo alive at the end of 1890, less than six months after he arrived. For the rest of his life his health suffered from the after-effects.

More profound than the physical ailments was the scarring on his soul from what he had seen. The secretive efforts of King Leopold's collaborators had successfully concealed the true nature of the Congo Free State from the outside world, making the reality of its brutal oppression and wanton pillage all the more shocking to an outsider like Conrad.

It would be eight years until he began writing *Heart of Darkness* and all the key details of his own Congo experience were included in the story told by Marlow. Marlow does not name the place as the Congo, or even the continent as Africa, but he describes how he was hired by European agents of a colonial company and sent to a river with a long, navigable reach through wild rainforest, that was only accessible by route march from the coast and which culminated in a remote 'Inner Station' home to the most profitable of all the company's ivory-collecting agents. In Conrad's early drafts the agent had the same name as the dying man Conrad tried to rescue in 1890, Mr Klein. The name in the novel was only later changed to Mr Kurtz.

But while it was written around facts Conrad knew to be true from his own experience, the power of *Heart of Darkness* comes from what Conrad adds. In his 1917 author's note, Conrad described how *Heart of Darkness* was more than the exercise of memory represented by *Youth*.

*Heart of Darkness* is experience, too; but it is experience pushed a little (and only very little) beyond the actual facts of the case for the perfectly legitimate, I believe, purpose of bringing it home to the minds and bosoms of the readers. There it was no longer a matter of sincere colouring. It was like another art altogether. That sombre theme had to be given a sinister resonance, a tonality of its own, a continued vibration that, I hoped, would hang in the air and dwell on the ear after the last note had been struck.

It is in the character of Mr Kurtz – the mysterious figure whose moral compass has apparently gone haywire upriver deep in the jungle – that Conrad's art reaches its highest form. People have sought the individual on whom Conrad based Mr Kurtz but the character is not a portrait of a single person. Instead, Mr Kurtz is a composite that includes elements of the acquisitive Belgian King, Leopold, and Henry Morton Stanley, the chancer-turned-explorer, who was hired by the king to stake the Congo, and a number of other colonial pioneers. But the most powerful feature of Mr Kurtz is that he includes elements of us all, characteristics of weakness, venality and arrogance that we can identify in ourselves. As a work of art, he is a masterpiece.

*Heart of Darkness* was written at the dawn of the colonial era in Africa and part of its power clearly comes from its eloquent denunciation of the conceit behind colonialism. But the real power of the book comes from its harrowing and often ambiguous account of humanity's moral decay. The lack of integrity of outsiders' values, their guilt and complicity are all offered up by Marlow as he struggles to distinguish between memories of his time on the river and subsequent nightmares, and the reality that his struggle has no clear, unequivocal conclusion makes reading *Heart of Darkness* today as richly rewarding as it was in the Edwardian era. To continue Conrad's musical metaphor, *Heart of Darkness* is more score than manuscript and just as no two performances of the same musical score are alike, no two readings of *Heart of Darkness* prompt exactly the same reaction.

Tim Butcher, Author of *Blood River: A Journey to Africa's Broken Heart* (Chatto & Windus, 2007)

# HEART OF DARKNESS

# HEART OF DARKNESS

## I

THE *Nellie*, a cruising yawl, swung to her anchor without a flutter of the sails, and was at rest. The flood had made, the wind was nearly calm, and being bound down the river, the only thing for it was to come to and wait for the turn of the tide.

The sea-reach of the Thames stretched before us like the beginning of an interminable waterway. In the offing the sea and the sky were welded together without a joint, and in the luminous space the tanned sails of the barges drifting up with the tide seemed to stand still in red clusters of canvas sharply peaked, with gleams of varnished spirits. A haze rested on the low shores that ran out to sea in vanishing flatness. The air was dark above Gravesend, and farther back still seemed condensed into a mournful gloom, brooding motionless over the biggest, and the greatest, town on earth.

The Director of Companies was our captain and our host. We four affectionately watched his back as he stood in the bows looking to seaward. On the whole river there was nothing that looked half so nautical. He resembled a pilot, which to a seaman is trustworthiness personified. It was difficult to realize his work was not out there in the luminous estuary, but behind him, within the brooding gloom.

Between us there was, as I have already said somewhere, the bond of the sea. Besides holding our hearts together through long periods of separation, it had the effect of making us tolerant of each other's yarns – and

3

even convictions. The Lawyer – the best of old fellows
– had, because of his many years and many virtues, the
only cushion on deck, and was lying on the only rug.
The Accountant had brought out already a box of dominoes, and was toying architecturally with the bones.
Marlow sat cross-legged right aft, leaning against the
mizzen-mast. He had sunken cheeks, a yellow complexion, a straight back, an ascetic aspect, and, with his arms
dropped, the palms of hands outwards, resembled an
idol. The Director, satisfied the anchor had good hold,
made his way aft and sat down amongst us. We exchanged a few words lazily. Afterwards there was silence
on board the yacht. For some reason or other we did not
begin that game of dominoes. We felt meditative, and
fit for nothing but placid staring. The day was ending
in a serenity of still and exquisite brilliance. The water
shone pacifically; the sky, without a speck, was a benign
immensity of unstained light; the very mist on the Essex
marshes was like a gauzy and radiant fabric, hung from
the wooded rises inland, and draping the low shores in
diaphanous folds. Only the gloom to the west, brooding over the upper reaches, became more sombre every
minute, as if angered by the approach of the sun.

And at last, in its curved and imperceptible fall, the
sun sank low, and from glowing white changed to a dull
red without rays and without heat, as if about to go out
suddenly, stricken to death by the touch of that gloom
brooding over a crowd of men.

Forthwith a change came over the waters, and the
serenity became less brilliant but more profound. The
old river in its broad reach rested unruffled at the de-
cline of day, after ages of good service done to the race
that peopled its banks, spread out in the tranquil dignity
of a waterway leading to the uttermost ends of the earth.
We looked at the venerable stream not in the vivid flush
of a short day that comes and departs for ever, but in the
august light of abiding memories. And indeed nothing

is easier for a man who has, as the phrase goes, "followed the sea" with reverence and affection, than to evoke the great spirit of the past upon the lower reaches of the Thames. The tidal current runs to and fro in its unceasing service, crowded with memories of men and ships it had borne to the rest of home or to the battles of the sea. It had known and served all the men of whom the nation is proud, from Sir Francis Drake to Sir John Franklin, knights all, titled and untitled – the great knights-errant of the sea. It had borne all the ships whose names are like jewels flashing in the night of time, from the *Golden Hind* returning with her round flanks full of treasure, to be visited by the Queen's Highness and thus pass out of the gigantic tale, to the *Erebus* and *Terror*, bound on other conquests – and that never returned. It had known the ships and the men. They had sailed from Deptford, from Greenwich, from Erith – the adventurers and the settlers; kings' ships and the ships of men on 'Change; captains, admirals, the dark "interlopers" of the Eastern trade, and the commissioned "generals" of East India fleets. Hunters for gold or pursuers of fame, they all had gone out on that stream, bearing the sword, and often the torch, messengers of the might within the land, bearers of a spark from the sacred fire. What greatness had not floated on the ebb of that river into the mystery of an unknown earth! . . . The dreams of men, the seed of commonwealths, the germs of empires.

The sun set; the dusk fell on the stream, and lights began to appear along the shore. The Chapman lighthouse, a three-legged thing erect on a mud-flat, shone strongly. Lights of ships moved in the fairway – a great stir of lights going up and going down. And farther west on the upper reaches the place of the monstrous town was still marked ominously on the sky, a brooding gloom in sunshine, a lurid glare under the stars.

"And this also," said Marlow suddenly, "has been one of the dark places of the earth."

He was the only man of us who still "followed the sea". The worst that could be said of him was that he did not represent his class. He was a seaman, but he was a wanderer, too, while most seamen lead, if one may so express it, a sedentary life. Their minds are of the stay-at-home order, and their home is always with them – the ship; and so is their country – the sea. One ship is very much like another, and the sea is always the same. In the immutability of their surroundings the foreign shores, the foreign faces, the changing immensity of life, glide past, veiled not by a sense of mystery but by a slightly disdainful ignorance; for there is nothing mysterious to a seaman unless it be the sea itself, which is the mistress of his existence and as inscrutable as Destiny. For the rest, after his hours of work, a casual stroll or a casual spree on shore suffices to unfold for him the secret of a whole continent, and generally he finds the secret not worth knowing. The yarns of seamen have a direct simplicity, the whole meaning of which lies within the shell of a cracked nut. But Marlow was not typical (if his propensity to spin yarns be excepted), and to him the meaning of an episode was not inside like a kernel but outside, enveloping the tale which brought it out only as a glow brings out a haze, in the likeness of one of these misty halos that sometimes are made visible by the spectral illumination of moonshine.

His remark did not seem at all surprising. It was just like Marlow. It was accepted in silence. No one took the trouble to grunt even; and presently he said, very slow –

"I was thinking of very old times, when the Romans first came here, nineteen hundred years ago – the other day . . . Light came out of this river since – you say Knights? Yes; but it is like a running blaze on a plain, like a flash of lightning in the clouds. We live in the flicker – may it last as long as the old earth keeps rolling! But darkness was here yesterday. Imagine the feelings of a commander of a fine – what d'ye call 'em? – trireme

in the Mediterranean, ordered suddenly to the north;
run overland across the Gauls in a hurry; put in charge
of one of these craft the legionaries – a wonderful lot of
handy men they must have been, too – used to build,
apparently by the hundred, in a month or two, if we may
believe what we read. Imagine him here – the very end
of the world, a sea the colour of lead, a sky the colour of
smoke, a kind of ship about as rigid as a concertina – and
going up this river with stores, or orders, or what you
like. Sand-banks, marshes, forests, savages, – precious
little to eat fit for a civilized man, nothing but Thames
water to drink. No Falernian wine here, no going ashore.
Here and there a military camp lost in a wilderness, like
a needle in a bundle of hay – cold, fog, tempests, disease, exile, and death – death skulking in the air, in the
water, in the bush. They must have been dying like flies
here. Oh, yes – he did it. Did it very well, too, no doubt,
and without thinking much about it either, except afterwards to brag of what he had gone through in his time,
perhaps. They were men enough to face the darkness.
And perhaps he was cheered by keeping his eye on a
chance of promotion to the fleet at Ravenna by-and-by,
if he had good friends in Rome and survived the awful
climate. Or think of a decent young citizen in a toga –
perhaps too much dice, you know – coming out here in
the train of some prefect, or tax-gatherer, or trader even,
to mend his fortunes. Land in a swamp, march through
the woods, and in some inland post feel the savagery,
the utter savagery, had closed round him, – all that mysterious life of the wilderness that stirs in the forest, in
the jungles, in the hearts of wild men. There's no initiation either into such mysteries. He has to live in the
midst of the incomprehensible, which is also detestable.
And it has a fascination, too, that goes to work upon him.
The fascination of the abomination – you know, imagine
the growing regrets, the longing to escape, the powerless disgust, the surrender, the hate."

He paused.

"Mind," he began again, lifting one arm from the elbow, the palm of the hand outwards, so that, with his legs folded before him, he had the pose of a Buddha preaching in European clothes and without a lotus-flower – "Mind, none of us would feel exactly like this. What saves us is efficiency – the devotion to efficiency. But these chaps were not much account, really. They were no colonists; their administration was merely a squeeze, and nothing more, I suspect. They were conquerors, and for that you want only brute force – nothing to boast of, when you have it, since your strength is just an accident arising from the weakness of others. They grabbed what they could get for the sake of what was to be got. It was just robbery with violence, aggravated murder on a great scale, and men going at it blind – as is very proper for those who tackle a darkness. The conquest of the earth, which mostly means the taking it away from those who have a different complexion or slightly flatter noses than ourselves, is not a pretty thing when you look into it too much. What redeems it is the idea only. An idea at the back of it; not a sentimental pretence but an idea; and an unselfish belief in the idea – something you can set up, and bow down before, and offer a sacrifice to . . ."

He broke off. Flames glided in the river, small green flames, red flames, white flames, pursuing, overtaking, joining, crossing each other – then separating slowly or hastily. The traffic of the great city went on in the deepening night upon the sleepless river. We looked on, waiting patiently – there was nothing else to do till the end of the flood; but it was only after a long silence, when he said, in a hesitating voice, "I suppose you fellows remember I did once turn fresh-water sailor for a bit", that we knew we were fated, before the ebb began to run, to hear about one of Marlow's inconclusive experiences.

"I don't want to bother you much with what happened

to me personally," he began, showing in this remark the
weakness of many tellers of tales who seem so often
unaware of what their audience would best like to hear;
"yet to understand the effect of it on me you ought to
know how I got out there, what I saw, how I went up
that river to the place where I first met the poor chap.
It was the farthest point of navigation and the culminat-
ing point of my experience. It seemed somehow to throw
a kind of light on everything about me – and into my
thoughts. It was sombre enough, too – and pitiful – not
extraordinary in any way – not very clear either. No, not
very clear. And yet it seemed to throw a kind of light.

"I had then, as you remember, just returned to London after a lot of Indian Ocean, Pacific, China Seas – a
regular dose of the East – six years or so, and I was loaf-
ing about, hindering you fellows in your work and invading your homes, just as though I had got a heavenly
mission to civilize you. It was very fine for a time, but
after a bit I did get tired of resting. Then I began to look
for a ship – I should think the hardest work on earth.
But the ships wouldn't even look at me. And I got tired
of that game, too.

"Now when I was a little chap I had a passion for
maps. I would look for hours at South America, or Africa,
or Australia, and lose myself in all the glories of explora-
tion. At that time there were many blank spaces on
the earth, and when I saw one that looked particularly
inviting on a map (but they all look that) I would put
my finger on it and say, When I grow up I will go there.
The North Pole was one of these places, I remember.
Well, I haven't been there yet, and shall not try now.
The glamour's off. Other places were scattered about
the Equator, and in every sort of latitude all over the two
hemispheres. I have been in some of them, and . . . well,
we won't talk about that. But there was one yet – the
biggest, the most blank, so to speak – that I had a hanker-
ing after.

"True, by this time it was not a blank space any more. It had got filled since my boyhood with rivers and lakes and names. It had ceased to be a blank space of delightful mystery – a white patch for a boy to dream gloriously over. It had become a place of darkness. But there was in it one river especially, a mighty big river, that you could see on the map, resembling an immense snake uncoiled, with its head in the sea, its body at rest curving afar over a vast country, and its tail lost in the depths of the land. And as I looked at the map of it in a shop-window, it fascinated me as a snake would a bird – a silly little bird. Then I remembered there was a big concern, a Company for trade on that river. Dash it all! I thought to myself, they can't trade without using some kind of craft on that lot of fresh water – steamboats! Why shouldn't I try to get charge of one? I went on along Fleet Street, but could not shake off the idea. The snake had charmed me.

"You understand it was a Continental concern, that Trading society; but I have a lot of relations living on the Continent, because it's cheap and not so nasty as it looks, they say.

"I am sorry to own I began to worry them. This was already a fresh departure for me. I was not used to get things that way, you know. I always went my own road and on my own legs where I had a mind to go. I wouldn't have believed it of myself; but, then – you see – I felt somehow I must get there by hook or by crook. So I worried them. The men said 'My dear fellow', and did nothing. Then – would you believe it? – I tried the women. I, Charlie Marlow, set the women to work – to get a job. Heavens! Well, you see, the notion drove me. I had an aunt, a dear enthusiastic soul. She wrote: 'It will be delightful. I am ready to do anything, anything for you. It is a glorious idea. I know the wife of a very high personage in the Administration, and also a man who has lots of influence with,' etc., etc. She was determined to make no end of fuss to get me appointed skipper of a river steamboat, if such was my fancy.

"I got my appointment – of course; and I got it very quick. It appears the Company had received news that one of their captains had been killed in a scuffle with the natives. This was my chance, and it made me the more anxious to go. It was only months and months afterwards, when I made the attempt to recover what was left of the body, that I heard the original quarrel arose from a misunderstanding about some hens. Yes, two black hens. Fresleven – that was the fellow's name, a Dane – thought himself wronged somehow in the bargain, so he went ashore and started to hammer the chief of the village with a stick. Oh, it didn't surprise me in the least to hear this, and at the same time to be told that Fresleven was the gentlest, quietest creature that ever walked on two legs. No doubt he was; but he had been a couple of years already out there engaged in the noble cause, you know, and he probably felt the need at last of asserting his self-respect in some way. Therefore he whacked the old nigger mercilessly, while a big crowd of his people watched him, thunderstruck, till some man – I was told the chief's son – in desperation at hearing the old chap yell, made a tentative jab with a spear at the white man – and of course it went quite easy between the shoulder-blades. Then the whole population cleared into the forest, expecting all kinds of calamities to happen, while, on the other hand, the steamer Fresleven commanded left also in a bad panic, in charge of the engineer, I believe. Afterwards nobody seemed to trouble much about Fresleven's remains, till I got out and stepped into his shoes. I couldn't let it rest, though; but when an opportunity offered at last to meet my predecessor, the grass growing through his ribs was tall enough to hide his bones. They were all there. The supernatural being had not been touched after he fell. And the village was deserted, the huts

gaped black, rotting, all askew within the fallen enclos-
ures. A calamity had come to it, sure enough. The
people had vanished. Mad terror had scattered them,
men, women, and children, through the bush, and they
had never returned. What became of the hens I don't
know either. I should think the cause of progress got
them, anyhow. However, through this glorious affair I
got my appointment, before I had fairly begun to hope
for it.

"I flew around like mad to get ready, and before forty-
eight hours I was crossing the Channel to show myself
to my employers, and sign the contract. In a very few
hours I arrived in a city that always makes me think of
a whited sepulchre. Prejudice no doubt. I had no difficulty in finding the Company's offices. It was the biggest thing in the town, and everybody I met was full of
it. They were going to run an over-sea empire, and make
no end of coin by trade.

"A narrow and deserted street in deep shadow, high
houses, innumerable windows with venetian blinds, a
dead silence, grass sprouting between the stones, imposing carriage archways right and left, immense double
doors standing ponderously ajar. I slipped through one
of these cracks, went up a swept and ungarnished stair-
case, as arid as a desert, and opened the first door I came
to. Two women, one fat and the other slim, sat on straw-
bottomed chairs, knitting black wool. The slim one got
up and walked straight at me – still knitting with down-
cast eyes – and only just as I began to think of getting
out of her way, as you would for a somnambulist, stood
still, and looked up. Her dress was as plain as an um-
brella-cover, and she turned round without a word and
preceded me into a waiting-room. I gave my name, and
looked about. Deal table in the middle, plain chairs all
round the walls, on one end a large shining map, marked
with all the colours of a rainbow. There was a vast
amount of red – good to see at any time, because one

knows that some real work is done in there, a deuce of
a lot of blue, a little green, smears of orange, and, on the
East Coast, a purple patch, to show where the jolly pioneers of progress drink the jolly lager-beer. However, I
wasn't going into any of these. I was going into the yellow. Dead in the centre. And the river was there – fascinating – deadly – like a snake. Ough! A door opened,
a white-haired secretarial head, but wearing a compassionate expression, appeared, and a skinny forefinger
beckoned me into the sanctuary. Its light was dim, and
a heavy writing-desk squatted in the middle. From behind that structure came out an impression of pale
plumpness in a frock-coat. The great man himself. He
was five feet six, I should judge, and had his grip on
the handle-end of ever so many millions. He shook
hands, I fancy, murmured vaguely, was satisfied with my
French. *Bon voyage*.

"In about forty-five seconds I found myself again
in the waiting-room with the compassionate secretary,
who, full of desolation and sympathy, made me sign
some document. I believe I undertook amongst other
things not to disclose any trade secrets. Well, I am not
going to.

"I began to feel slightly uneasy. You know I am not
used to such ceremonies, and there was something ominous in the atmosphere. It was just as though I had
been let into some conspiracy – I don't know – something not quite right; and I was glad to get out. In the
outer room the two women knitted black wool feverish-
ly. People were arriving, and the younger one was walking back and forth introducing them. The old one sat
on her chair. Her flat cloth slippers were propped up on
a foot-warmer, and a cat reposed on her lap. She wore a
starched white affair on her head, had a wart on one
cheek, and silver-rimmed spectacles hung on the tip of
her nose. She glanced at me above the glasses. The swift
and indifferent placidity of that look troubled me. Two

youths with foolish and cheery countenances were being piloted over, and she threw at them the same quick glance of unconcerned wisdom. She seemed to know all about them and about me, too. An eerie feeling came over me. She seemed uncanny and fateful. Often far away there I thought of these two, guarding the door of Darkness, knitting black wool as for a warm pall, one introducing, introducing continuously to the unknown, the other scrutinizing the cheery and foolish faces with unconcerned old eyes. *Ave!* Old knitter of black wool. *Morituri te salutant.* Not many of those she looked at ever saw her again – not half, by a long way.

"There was yet a visit to the doctor. 'A simple formality,' assured me the secretary, with an air of taking an immense part in all my sorrows. Accordingly a young chap wearing his hat over the left eyebrow, some clerk I suppose – there must have been clerks in the business, though the house was as still as a house in a city of the dead – came from somewhere up-stairs, and led me forth. He was shabby and careless, with ink-stains on the sleeves of his jacket, and his cravat was large and billowy, under a chin shaped like the toe of an old boot. It was a little too early for the doctor, so I proposed a drink, and thereupon he developed a vein of joviality. As we sat over our vermouths he glorified the Company's business, and by-and-by I expressed casually my surprise at him not going out there. He became very cool and collected all at once. 'I am not such a fool as I look, quoth Plato to his disciples,' he said sententiously, emptied his glass with great resolution, and we rose.

"The old doctor felt my pulse, evidently thinking of something else the while. 'Good, good for there,' he mumbled, and then with a certain eagerness asked me whether I would let him measure my head. Rather surprised, I said Yes, when he produced a thing like calipers and got the dimensions back and front and every way, taking notes carefully. He was an unshaven little man in

a threadbare coat like a gaberdine, with his feet in slippers, and I thought him a harmless fool. 'I always ask
leave, in the interests of science, to measure the crania
of those going out there,' he said. 'And when they come
back, too?' I asked. 'Oh, I never see them,' he remarked;
'and, moreover, the changes take place inside, you
know.' He smiled, as if at some quiet joke. 'So you are
going out there. Famous. Interesting, too.' He gave me
a searching glance, and made another note. 'Ever any
madness in your family?' he asked, in a matter-of-fact
tone. I felt very annoyed. 'Is that question in the interests of science, too?' 'It would be,' he said, without taking notice of my irritation, 'interesting for science to
watch the mental changes of individuals, on the spot,
but . . .' 'Are you an alienist?' I interrupted. 'Every doctor should be – a little,' answered that original, imper-
turbably. 'I have a little theory which you Messieurs who
go out there must help me to prove. This is my share in
the advantages my country shall reap from the possession of such a magnificent dependency. The mere wealth
I leave to others. Pardon my questions, but you are the
first Englishman coming under my observation . . .' I
hastened to assure him I was not in the least typical. 'If
I were,' said I, 'I wouldn't be talking like this with you.'
'What you say is rather profound, and probably erro-
neous,' he said, with a laugh. 'Avoid irritation more than
exposure to the sun. Adieu. How do you English say, eh?
Good-bye. Ah! Good-bye. Adieu. In the tropics one must
before everything keep calm.' . . . He lifted a warning
forefinger . . . '*Du calme, du calme. Adieu.*'

"One thing more remained to do – say good-bye to
my excellent aunt. I found her triumphant. I had a cup
of tea – the last decent cup of tea for many days – and
in a room that most soothingly looked just as you would
expect a lady's drawing-room to look, we had a long
quiet chat by the fireside. In the course of these
confidences it became quite plain to me I had been

represented to the wife of the high dignitary, and goodness knows to how many more people besides, as an
exceptional and gifted creature – a piece of good fortune
for the Company – a man you don't get hold of every
day. Good heavens! and I was going to take charge of a
two-penny-half-penny river-steamboat with a penny
whistle attached! It appeared, however, I was also one
of the Workers, with a capital – you know. Something
like an emissary of light, something like a lower sort of
apostle. There had been a lot of such rot let loose in
print and talk just about that time, and the excellent
woman, living right in the rush of all that humbug, got
carried off her feet. She talked about 'weaning those
ignorant millions from their horrid ways', till, upon my
word, she made me quite uncomfortable. I ventured to
hint that the Company was run for profit.

" 'You forget, dear Charlie, that the labourer is worthy
of his hire,' she said, brightly. It's queer how out of touch
with truth women are. They live in a world of their own,
and there had never been anything like it, and never
can be. It is too beautiful altogether, and if they were to
set it up it would go to pieces before the first sunset.
Some confounded fact we men have been living con-
tentedly with ever since the day of creation would start
up and knock the whole thing over.

"After this I got embraced, told to wear flannel, be
sure to write often, and so on – and I left. In the street
– I don't know why – a queer feeling came to me that I
was an imposter. Odd thing that I, who used to clear out
for any part of the world at twenty-four hours' notice,
with less thought than most men give to the crossing of
a street, had a moment – I won't say of hesitation, but
of startled pause, before this commonplace affair. The
best way I can explain it to you is by saying that, for a
second or two, I felt as though, instead of going to the
centre of a continent, I were about to set off for the centre
of the earth.

"I left in a French steamer, and she called in every blamed port they have out there, for, as far as I could see, the sole purpose of landing soldiers and custom-house officers. I watched the coast. Watching a coast as it slips by the ship is like thinking about an enigma. There it is before you – smiling, frowning, inviting, grand, mean, insipid, or savage, and always mute with an air of whispering, Come and find out. This one was almost featureless, as if still in the making, with an aspect of monotonous grimness. The edge of a colossal jungle, so dark-green as to be almost black, fringed with white surf, ran straight, like a ruled line, far, far away along a blue sea whose glitter was blurred by a creeping mist. The sun was fierce, the land seemed to glisten and drip with steam. Here and there grayish-whitish specks showed up clustered inside the white surf, with a flag flying above them perhaps. Settlements some centuries old, and still no bigger than pinheads on the untouched expanse of their background. We pounded along, stopped, landed soldiers; went on, landed custom-house clerks to levy toll in what looked like a God-forsaken wilderness, with a tin shed and a flag-pole lost in it; landed more soldiers – to take care of the custom-house clerks, presumably. Some, I heard, got drowned in the surf; but whether they did or not, nobody seemed particularly to care. They were just flung out there, and on we went. Every day the coast looked the same, as though we had not moved; but we passed various places – trading places – with names like Gran' Bassam, Little Popo; names that seemed to belong to some sordid farce acted in front of a sinister back-cloth. The idleness of a passenger, my isolation amongst all these men with whom I had no point of contact, the oily and languid sea, the uniform sombreness of the coast, seemed to keep me away from the truth of things, within the toil of a mournful and senseless delusion. The voice of the surf heard now and then was a positive pleasure, like the

speech of a brother. It was something natural, that had
its reason, that had a meaning. Now and then a boat from
the shore gave one a momentary contact with reality. It
was paddled by black fellows. You could see from afar
the white of their eyeballs glistening. They shouted,
sang; their bodies streamed with perspiration; they had
faces like grotesque masks – these chaps; but they
had bone, muscle, a wild vitality, an intense energy of
movement, that was as natural and true as the surf along
their coast. They wanted no excuse for being there.
They were a great comfort to look at. For a time I would
feel I belonged still to a world of straightforward facts;
but the feeling would not last long. Something would
turn up to scare it away. Once, I remember, we came
upon a man-of-war anchored off the coast. There wasn't
even a shed there, and she was shelling the bush. It
appears the French had one of their wars going on thereabouts. Her ensign dropped limp like a rag; the muzzles
of the long six-inch guns stuck out all over the low hull;
the greasy, slimy swell swung her up lazily and let her
down, swaying her thin masts. In the empty immensity
of earth, sky, and water, there she was, incomprehensible, firing into a continent. Pop, would go one of the
six-inch guns; a small flame would dart and vanish,
a little white smoke would disappear, a tiny projectile
would give a feeble screech – and nothing happened.
Nothing could happen. There was a touch of insanity
in the proceeding, a sense of lugubrious drollery in the
sight; and it was not dissipated by somebody on board
assuring me earnestly there was a camp of natives – he
called them enemies! – hidden out of sight somewhere.

"We gave her her letters (I heard the men in that lonely ship were dying of fever at the rate of three a-day)
and went on. We called at some more places with farcical
names, where the merry dance of death and trade goes
on in a still and earthy atmosphere as of an overheated
catacomb; all along the formless coast bordered by dan-

gerous surf, as if Nature herself had tried to ward off
intruders; in and out of rivers, streams of death in life,
whose banks were rotting into mud, whose waters,
thickened into slime, invaded the contorted mangroves,
that seemed to writhe at us in the extremity of an im-
potent despair. Nowhere did we stop long enough to get
a particularized impression, but the general sense of
vague and oppressive wonder grew upon me. It was like
a weary pilgrimage amongst hints for nightmares.

"It was upward of thirty days before I saw the mouth
of the big river. We anchored off the seat of the government. But my work would not begin till some two hundred miles farther on. So as soon as I could I made a start
for a place thirty miles higher up.

"I had my passage on a little sea-going steamer. Her
captain was a Swede, and knowing me for a seaman,
invited me on the bridge. He was a young man, lean,
fair, and morose, with lanky hair and a shuffling gait. As
we left the miserable little wharf, he tossed his head
contemptuously at the shore. 'Been living there?' he
asked. I said, 'Yes.' 'Fine lot these government chaps –
are they not?' he went on, speaking English with great
precision and considerable bitterness. 'It is funny what
some people will do for a few francs a-month. I wonder
what becomes of that kind when it goes up country?' I
said to him I expected to see that soon. 'So-o-o!' he exclaimed. He shuffled athwart, keeping one eye ahead
vigilantly. 'Don't be too sure,' he continued. 'The other
day I took up a man who hanged himself on the road.
He was a Swede, too.' 'Hanged himself! Why, in God's
name?' I cried. He kept on looking out watchfully. 'Who
knows? The sun too much for him, or the country
perhaps.'

"At last we opened a reach. A rocky cliff appeared,
mounds of turned-up earth by the shore, houses on a
hill, others with iron roofs, amongst a waste of excava-
tions, or hanging to the declivity. A continuous noise of

the rapids above hovered over this scene of inhabited
devastation. A lot of people, mostly black and naked,
moved about like ants. A jetty projected into the river.
A blinding sunlight drowned all this at times in a sudden
recrudescence of glare. 'There's your Company's station,' said the Swede, pointing to three wooden barrack-
like structures on the rocky slope. 'I will send your
things up. Four boxes did you say? So. Farewell.'

"I came upon a boiler wallowing in the grass, then
found a path leading up the hill. It turned aside for the
boulders, and also for an undersized railway-truck lying
there on its back with its wheels in the air. One was off.
The thing looked as dead as the carcass of some animal.
I came upon more pieces of decaying machinery, a stack
of rusty rails. To the left a clump of trees made a shady
spot, where dark things seemed to stir feebly. I blinked,
the path was steep. A horn tooted to the right, and I saw
the black people run. A heavy and dull detonation
shook the ground, a puff of smoke came out of the cliff,
and that was all. No change appeared on the face of the
rock. They were building a railway. The cliff was not in
the way or anything; but this objectless blasting was all
the work going on.

"A slight clinking behind me made me turn my head.
Six black men advanced in a file, toiling up the path.
They walked erect and slow, balancing small baskets
full of earth on their heads, and the clink kept time with
their footsteps. Black rags were wound round their loins,
and the short ends behind waggled to and fro like tails.
I could see every rib, the joints of their limbs were like
knots in a rope; each had an iron collar on his neck, and
all were connected together with a chain whose bights
swung between them, rhythmically clinking. Another
report from the cliff made me think suddenly of that
ship of war I had seen firing into a continent. It was the
same kind of ominous voice; but these men could by no
stretch of imagination be called enemies. They were

called criminals, and the outraged law, like the bursting shells, had come to them, an insoluble mystery from the sea. All their meagre breasts panted together, the violently dilated nostrils quivered, the eyes stared stonily up-hill. They passed me within six inches, without a glance, with that complete, deathlike indifference of unhappy savages. Behind this raw matter one of the reclaimed, the product of the new forces at work, strolled despondently, carrying a rifle by its middle. He had a uniform jacket with one button off, and seeing a white man on the path, hoisted his weapon to his shoulder with alacrity. This was simple prudence, white men being so much alike at a distance that he could not tell who I might be. He was speedily reassured, and with a large, white, rascally grin, and a glance at his charge, seemed to take me into partnership in his exalted trust. After all, I also was a part of the great cause of these high and just proceedings.

"Instead of going up, I turned and descended to the left. My idea was to let that chain-gang get out of sight before I climbed the hill. You know I am not particularly tender; I've had to strike and to fend off. I've had to resist and to attack sometimes – that's only one way of resisting – without counting the exact cost, according to the demands of such sort of life as I had blundered into. I've seen the devil of violence, and the devil of greed, and the devil of hot desire; but, by all the stars! these were strong, lusty, red-eyed devils, that swayed and drove men – men, I tell you. But as I stood on this hillside, I foresaw that in the blinding sunshine of that land I would become acquainted with a flabby, pretending, weak-eyed devil of a rapacious and pitiless folly. How insidious he could be, too, I was only to find out several months later and a thousand miles farther. For a moment I stood appalled, as though by a warning. Finally I descended the hill, obliquely, towards the trees I had seen.

"I avoided a vast artificial hole somebody had been

digging on the slope, the purpose of which I found it impossible to divine. It wasn't a quarry or a sandpit, anyhow. It was just a hole. It might have been connected with the philanthropic desire of giving the criminals something to do. I don't know. Then I nearly fell into a very narrow ravine, almost no more than a scar in the hillside. I discovered that a lot of imported drainage-pipes for the settlement had been tumbled in there. There wasn't one that was not broken. It was a wanton smash-up. At last I got under the trees. My purpose was to stroll into the shade for a moment; but no sooner within than it seemed to me I had stepped into the gloomy circle of some Inferno. The rapids were near, and an uninterrupted, uniform, headlong, rushing noise filled the mournful stillness of the grove, where not a breath stirred, not a leaf moved, with a mysterious sound – as though the tearing pace of the launched earth had suddenly become audible.

"Black shapes crouched, lay, sat between the trees leaning against the trunks, clinging to the earth, half coming out, half effaced within the dim light, in all the attitudes of pain, abandonment, and despair. Another mine on the cliff went off, followed by a slight shudder of the soil under my feet. The work was going on. The work! And this was the place where some of the helpers had withdrawn to die.

"They were dying slowly – it was very clear. They were not enemies, they were not criminals, they were nothing earthly now, – nothing but black shadows of disease and starvation, lying confusedly in the greenish gloom. Brought from all the recesses of the coast in all the legality of time contracts, lost in uncongenial surroundings, fed on unfamiliar food, they sickened, became inefficient, and were then allowed to crawl away and rest. These moribund shapes were free as air – and nearly as thin. I began to distinguish the gleam of the eyes under the trees. Then, glancing down, I saw a

face near my hand. The black bones reclined at full
length with one shoulder against the tree, and slowly
the eyelids rose and the sunken eyes looked up at me,
enormous and vacant, a kind of blind, white flicker in
the depths of the orbs, which died out slowly. The man
seemed young – almost a boy – but you know with them
it's hard to tell. I found nothing else to do but to offer
him one of my good Swede's ship's biscuits I had in my
pocket. The fingers closed slowly on it and held – there
was no other movement and no other glance. He had
tied a bit of white worsted round his neck – Why? Where
did he get it? Was it a badge – an ornament – a charm –
a propitiatory act? Was there any idea at all connected
with it? It looked startling round his black neck, this bit
of white thread from beyond the seas.

"Near the same tree two more bundles of acute
angles sat with their legs drawn up. One, with his chin
propped on his knees, stared at nothing, in an intolerable and appalling manner: his brother phantom rested
its forehead, as if overcome with a great weariness; and
all about others were scattered in every pose of contorted collapse, as in some picture of a massacre or a
pestilence. While I stood horror-struck, one of these
creatures rose to his hands and knees, and went off on
all-fours towards the river to drink. He lapped out of his
hand, then sat up in the sunlight, crossing his shins in
front of him, and after a time let his woolly head fall on
his breastbone.

"I didn't want any more loitering in the shade, and I
made haste towards the station. When near the buildings I met a white man, in such an unexpected elegance
of get-up that in the first moment I took him for a sort
of vision. I saw a high starched collar, white cuffs, a light
alpaca jacket, snowy trousers, a clear necktie, and varnished boots. No hat. Hair parted, brushed, oiled, under
a green-lined parasol held in a big white hand. He was
amazing, and had a penholder behind his ear.

"I shook hands with this miracle, and I learned he
was the Company's chief accountant, and that all the
book-keeping was done at this station. He had come out
for a moment, he said, 'to get a breath of fresh air'. The
expression sounded wonderfully odd, with its sugges-
tion of sedentary desk-life. I wouldn't have mentioned
the fellow to you at all, only it was from his lips that I
first heard the name of the man who is so indissolubly
connected with the memories of that time. Moreover, I
respected the fellow. Yes; I respected his collars, his vast
cuffs, his brushed hair. His appearance was certainly
that of a hairdresser's dummy; but in the great demor-
alization of the land he kept up his appearance. That's
backbone. His starched collars and got-up shirt-fronts
were achievements of character. He had been out nearly
three years; and, later, I could not help asking him how
he managed to sport such linen. He had just the faintest
blush, and said modestly, 'I've been teaching one of the
native women about the station. It was difficult. She had
a distaste for the work.' Thus this man had verily accomplished something. And he was devoted to his
books, which were in apple-pie order.

"Everything else in the station was in a muddle –
heads, things, buildings. Strings of dusty niggers with
splay feet arrived and departed; a stream of manufac-
tured goods, rubbishy cottons, beads, and brass-wire set
into the depths of darkness, and in return came a
precious trickle of ivory.

"I had to wait in the station for ten days – an eternity.
I lived in a hut in the yard, but to be out of the chaos I
would sometimes get into the accountant's office. It was
built of horizontal planks, and so badly put together
that, as he bent over his high desk, he was barred from
neck to heels with narrow strips of sunlight. There was
no need to open the big shutter to see. It was hot there,
too; big flies buzzed fiendishly, and did not sting, but
stabbed. I sat generally on the floor, while, of faultless

appearance (and even slightly scented), perching on a high stool, he wrote, he wrote. Sometimes he stood up for exercise. When a truckle-bed with a sick man (some invalid agent from up-country) was put in there, he exhibited a gentle annoyance. 'The groans of this sick person,' he said, 'distract my attention. And without that it is extremely difficult to guard against clerical errors in this climate.'

"One day he remarked, without lifting his head, 'In the interior you will no doubt meet Mr. Kurtz.' On my asking who Mr. Kurtz was, he said he was a first-class agent; and seeing my disappointment at this information, he added slowly, laying down his pen, 'He is a very remarkable person.' Further questions elicited from him that Mr. Kurtz was at present in charge of a trading post, a very important one, in the true ivory-country, at 'the very bottom of there. Sends in as much ivory as all the others put together . . . ' He began to write again. The sick man was too ill to groan. The flies buzzed in a great peace.

"Suddenly there was a growing murmur of voices and a great tramping of feet. A caravan had come in. A violent babble of uncouth sounds burst out on the other side of the planks. All the carriers were speaking together, and in the midst of the uproar the lamentable voice of the chief agent was heard 'giving it up' tearfully for the twentieth time that day. . . He rose slowly. 'What a frightful row,' he said. He crossed the room gently to look at the sick man, and returning, said to me, 'He does not hear.' 'What! Dead?' I asked, startled. 'No, not yet,' he answered, with great composure. Then, alluding with a toss of the head to the tumult in the station-yard, 'When one has got to make correct entries, one comes to hate those savages – hate them to the death.' He remained thoughtful for a moment. 'When you see Mr. Kurtz,' he went on, 'tell him from me that everything here' – he glanced at the desk – 'is very satisfactory. I

don't like to write to him – with those messengers of
ours you never know who may get hold of your letter –
at that Central Station.' He stared at me for a moment
with his mild, bulging eyes. 'Oh, he will go far, very far,'
he began again. 'He will be a somebody in the Administration before long. They, above – the Council in Europe, you know – mean him to be.'

"He turned to his work. The noise outside had
ceased, and presently in going out I stopped at the door.
In the steady buzz of flies the homeward-bound agent
was lying flushed and insensible; the other, bent over
his books, was making correct entries of perfectly correct transactions; and fifty feet below the doorstep I
could see the still tree-tops of the grove of death.

"Next day I left that station at last, with a caravan of
sixty men, for a two-hundred-mile tramp.

"No use telling you much about that. Paths, paths,
everywhere; a stamped-in network of paths spreading
over the empty land, through long grass, through burnt
grass, through thickets, down and up chilly ravines, up
and down stony hills ablaze with heat; and a solitude, a
solitude, nobody, not a hut. The population had cleared
out a long time ago. Well, if a lot of mysterious niggers
armed with all kinds of fearful weapons suddenly took
to travelling on the road between Deal and Gravesend,
catching the yokels right and left to carry heavy loads
for them, I fancy every farm and cottage thereabouts
would get empty very soon. Only here the dwellings
were gone, too. Still I passed through several abandoned
villages. There's something pathetically childish in the
ruins of grass walls. Day after day, with the stamp and
shuffle of sixty pair of bare feet behind me, each pair
under a 60-lb. load. Camp, cook, sleep, strike camp,
march. Now and then a carrier dead in harness, at rest
in the long grass near the path, with an empty water-
gourd and his long staff lying by his side. A great silence
around and above. Perhaps on some quiet night the

tremor of far-off drums, sinking, swelling, a tremor vast, faint; a sound weird, appealing, suggestive, and wild – and perhaps with as profound a meaning as the sound of bells in a Christian country. Once a white man in an unbuttoned uniform, camping on the path with an armed escort of lank Zanzibaris, very hospitable and festive – not to say drunk. Was looking after the upkeep of the road, he declared. Can't say I saw any road or any upkeep, unless the body of a middle-aged negro, with a bullet-hole in the forehead, upon which I absolutely stumbled three miles farther on, may be considered as a permanent improvement. I had a white companion, too, not a bad chap, but rather too fleshy and with the exasperating habit of fainting on the hot hillsides, miles away from the least bit of shade and water. Annoying, you know, to hold your own coat like a parasol over a man's head while he is coming-to. I couldn't help asking him once what he meant by coming there at all. 'To make money, of course. What do you think?' he said, scornfully. Then he got fever, and had to be carried in a hammock slung under a pole. As he weighed sixteen stone I had no end of rows with the carriers. They jibbed, ran away, sneaked off with their loads in the night – quite a mutiny. So, one evening, I made a speech in English with gestures, not one of which was lost to the sixty pairs of eyes before me, and the next morning I started the hammock off in front all right. An hour afterwards I came upon the whole concern wrecked in a bush – man, hammock, groans, blankets, horrors. The heavy pole had skinned his poor nose. He was very anxious for me to kill somebody, but there wasn't the shadow of a carrier near. I remember the old doctor, – 'It would be interesting for science to watch the mental changes of individuals, on the spot.' I felt I was becoming scientifically interesting. However, all that is to no purpose. On the fifteenth day I came in sight of the big river again, and hobbled into the Central Station. It was

on a backwater surrounded by scrub and forest, with a
pretty border of smelly mud on one side, and on the
three others enclosed by a crazy fence of rushes. A neglected gap was all the gate it had, and the first glance at
the place was enough to let you see the flabby devil was
running that show. White men with long staves in their
hands appeared languidly from amongst the buildings,
strolling up to take a look at me, and then retired out of
sight somewhere. One of them, a stout, excitable chap
with black moustaches, informed me with great volu-
bility and many digressions, as soon as I told him who I
was, that my steamer was at the bottom of the river. I
was thunderstruck. What, how, why? Oh, it was 'all
right'. The 'manager himself' was there. All quite correct. 'Everybody had behaved splendidly! splendidly!'
– 'you must,' he said in agitation, 'go and see the general
manager at once. He is waiting!'

"I did not see the real significance of that wreck at
once. I fancy I see it now, but I am not sure – not at all.
Certainly the affair was too stupid – when I think of it
– to be altogether natural. Still . . . But at the moment it
presented itself simply as a confounded nuisance. The
steamer was sunk. They had started two days before in
a sudden hurry up the river with the manager on board,
in charge of some volunteer skipper, and before they
had been out three hours they tore the bottom out of
her on stones, and she sank near the south bank. I asked
myself what I was to do there, now my boat was lost. As
a matter of fact, I had plenty to do in fishing my command out of the river. I had to set about it the very next
day. That, and the repairs when I brought the pieces to
the station, took some months.

"My first interview with the manager was curious. He
did not ask me to sit down after my twenty-mile walk
that morning. He was commonplace in complexion, in
feature, in manners, and in voice. He was of middle size
and of ordinary build. His eyes, of the usual blue, were

perhaps remarkably cold, and he certainly could make his glance fall on one as trenchant and heavy as an axe. But even at these times the rest of his person seemed to disclaim the intention. Otherwise there was only an indefinable, faint expression of his lips, something stealthy – a smile – not a smile – I remember it, but I can't explain. It was unconscious, this smile was, though just after he had said something it got intensified for an instant. It came at the end of his speeches like a seal applied on the words to make the meaning of the commonest phrase appear absolutely inscrutable. He was a common trader, from his youth up employed in these parts – nothing more. He was obeyed, yet he inspired neither love nor fear, nor even respect. He inspired uneasiness. That was it! Uneasiness. Not a definite mistrust – just uneasiness – nothing more. You have no idea how effective such a . . . a . . . faculty can be. He had no genius for organizing, for initiative, or for order even. That was evident in such things as the deplorable state of the station. He had no learning, and no intelligence. His position had come to him – why? Perhaps because he was never ill . . . He had served three terms of three years out there . . . Because triumphant health in the general rout of constitutions is a kind of power in itself. When he went home on leave he rioted on a large scale – pompously. Jack ashore – with a difference – in externals only. This one could gather from his casual talk. He originated nothing, he could keep the routine going – that's all. But he was great. He was great by this little thing that it was impossible to tell what could control such a man. He never gave that secret away. Perhaps there was nothing within him. Such a suspicion made one pause – for out there there were no external checks. Once when various tropical diseases had laid low almost every 'agent' in the station, he was heard to say, 'Men who come out here should have no entrails.' He sealed the utterance with that smile of his, as though it had been a door opening into a darkness he had in his keeping. You fancied you had seen things – but the seal was on. When annoyed at meal-times by the constant quarrels of the white men about precedence, he ordered an immense round table to be made, for which a special house had to be built. This was the station's mess-room. Where he sat was the first place – the rest were nowhere. One felt this to be his unalterable conviction. He was neither civil nor uncivil. He was quiet. He allowed his 'boy' – an overfed young negro from the coast – to treat the white men, under his very eyes, with provoking insolence.

"He began to speak as soon as he saw me. I had been very long on the road. He could not wait. Had to start without me. The up-river stations had to be relieved. There had been so many delays already that he did not know who was dead and who was alive, and how they got on – and so on, and so on. He paid no attention to my explanations, and, playing with a stick of sealing-wax, repeated several times that the situation was 'very grave, very grave'. There were rumours that a very important station was in jeopardy, and its chief, Mr. Kurtz, was ill. Hoped it was not true. Mr. Kurtz was . . . I felt weary and irritable. Hang Kurtz, I thought. I interrupted him by saying I had heard of Mr. Kurtz on the coast. 'Ah! So they talk of him down there,' he murmured to himself. Then he began again, assuring me Mr. Kurtz was the best agent he had, an exceptional man, of the greatest importance to the Company; therefore I could understand his anxiety. He was, he said, 'very, very uneasy'. Certainly he fidgeted on his chair a good deal, exclaimed, 'Ah, Mr. Kurtz!' broke the stick of sealing-wax and seemed dumbfounded by the accident. Next thing he wanted to know 'how long it would take to' . . . I interrupted him again. Being hungry, you know, and kept on my feet, too, I was getting savage. 'How could I tell?' I said. 'I hadn't even seen the wreck yet – some months, no doubt.' All this talk seemed to me so futile. 'Some months,' he said. 'Well, let us say three months before we can make a start. Yes. That ought to do the affair.' I flung out of his hut (he lived all alone in a clay hut with a sort of verandah) muttering to myself my opinion of him. He was a chattering idiot. Afterwards I took it back when it was borne in upon me startlingly with what extreme nicety he had estimated the time requisite for the 'affair'.

"I went to work the next day, turning, so to speak, my back on that station. In that way only it seemed to me I could keep my hold on the redeeming facts of life. Still, one must look about sometimes; and then I saw this station, these men strolling aimlessly about in the sunshine of the yard. I asked myself sometimes what it all meant. They wandered here and there with their absurd long staves in their hands, like a lot of faithless pilgrims bewitched inside a rotten fence. The word 'ivory' rang in the air, was whispered, was sighed. You would think they were praying to it. A taint of imbecile rapacity blew through it all, like a whiff from some corpse. By Jove! I've never seen anything so unreal in my life. And outside, the silent wilderness surrounding this cleared speck on the earth struck me as something great and invincible, like evil or truth, waiting patiently for the passing away of this fantastic invasion.

"Oh, these months! Well, never mind. Various things happened. One evening a grass shed full of calico, cotton prints, beads, and I don't know what else, burst into a blaze so suddenly that you would have thought the earth had opened to let an avenging fire consume all that trash. I was smoking my pipe quietly by my dismantled steamer, and saw them all cutting capers in the light, with their arms lifted high, when the stout man with moustaches came tearing down to the river, a tin pail in his hand, assured me that everybody was 'behaving splendidly, splendidly', dipped about a quart of water and tore back again. I noticed there was a hole in the bottom of his pail.

"I strolled up. There was no hurry. You see the thing had gone off like a box of matches. It had been hopeless from the very first. The flame had leaped high, driven everybody back, lighted up everything – and collapsed. The shed was already a heap of embers glowing fiercely. A nigger was being beaten near by. They said he had caused the fire in some way; be that as it may, he was screeching most horribly. I saw him, later, for several days, sitting in a bit of shade looking very sick and trying to recover himself: afterwards he arose and went out – and the wilderness without a sound took him into its bosom again. As I approached the glow from the dark I found myself at the back of two men, talking. I heard the name of Kurtz pronounced, then the words, 'take advantage of this unfortunate accident'. One of the men was the manager. I wished him a good evening. 'Did you ever see anything like it – eh? it is incredible,' he said, and walked off. The other man remained. He was a first-class agent, young, gentlemanly, a bit reserved, with a forked little beard and a hooked nose. He was stand-off-ish with the other agents, and they on their side said he was the manager's spy upon them. As to me, I had hardly ever spoken to him before. We got into talk, and by-and-by we strolled away from the hissing ruins. Then he asked me to his room, which was in the main building of the station. He struck a match, and I perceived that this young aristocrat had not only a silver-mounted dressing-case but also a whole candle all to himself. Just at that time the manager was the only man supposed to have any right to candles. Native mats covered the clay walls; a collection of spears, assegais, shields, knives was hung up in trophies. The business entrusted to this fellow was the making of bricks – so I had been informed; but there wasn't a fragment of a brick anywhere in the station, and he had been there more than a year – waiting. It seems he could not make bricks without something, I don't know what – straw maybe. Anyways, it could not be found there, and as it was not likely to be sent from Europe, it did not appear clear to me what he was waiting for. An act of special creation perhaps. However, they were all waiting – all the sixteen or twenty pilgrims of them – for something; and upon my word it did not seem an uncongenial occupation, from the way they took it, though the only thing that ever came to them was disease – as far as I could see. They beguiled the time by backbiting and intriguing against each other in a foolish kind of way. There was an air of plotting about that station, but nothing came of it, of course. It was as unreal as everything else – as the philanthropic pretence of the whole concern, as their talk, as their government, as their show of work. The only real feeling was a desire to get appointed to a trading-post where ivory was to be had, so that they could earn percentages. They intrigued and slandered and hated each other only on that account – but as to effectually lifting a little finger – oh, no. By heavens! there is something after all in the world allowing one man to steal a horse while another must not look at a halter. Steal a horse straight out. Very well. He has done it. Perhaps he can ride. But there is a way of looking at a halter that would provoke the most charitable of saints into a kick.

"I had no idea why he wanted to be sociable, but as we chatted in there it suddenly occurred to me the fellow was trying to get at something – in fact, pumping me. He alluded constantly to Europe, to the people I was supposed to know there – putting leading questions as to my acquaintances in the sepulchral city, and so on. His little eyes glittered like mica discs – with curiosity – though he tried to keep up a bit of superciliousness. At first I was astonished, but very soon I became awfully curious to see what he would find out from me. I couldn't possibly imagine what I had in me to make it worth his while. It was very pretty to see how he baffled himself, for in truth my body was full only of chills, and my head had nothing in it but that wretched steamboat business. It was evident he took me for a perfectly shameless prevaricator. At last he got angry, and, to conceal a movement of furious annoyance, he yawned. I rose. Then I noticed a small sketch in oils, on a panel, representing a woman, draped and blindfolded, carrying a lighted torch. The background was sombre – almost black. The movement of the woman was stately, and the effect of the torch-light on the face was sinister.

"It arrested me, and he stood by civilly, holding an empty half-pint champagne bottle (medical comforts) with the candle stuck in it. To my question he said Mr. Kurtz had painted this – in this very station more than a year ago – while waiting for means to go to his trading-post. 'Tell me, pray,' said I, 'who is this Mr. Kurtz?'

" 'The chief of the Inner Station,' he answered in a short tone, looking away. 'Much obliged,' I said, laughing. 'And you are the brickmaker of the Central Station. Everyone knows that.' He was silent for a while. 'He is a prodigy,' he said at last. 'He is an emissary of pity, and science, and progress, and devil knows what else. We want,' he began to declaim suddenly, 'for the guidance of the cause entrusted to us by Europe, so to speak, higher intelligence, wide sympathies, a singleness of purpose.' 'Who says that?' I asked. 'Lots of them,' he replied. 'Some even write that; and so *he* comes here, a special being, as you ought to know.' 'Why ought I to know?' I interrupted, really surprised. He paid no attention. 'Yes. Today he is chief of the best station, next year he will be assistant-manager, two years more and ... but I daresay you know what he will be in two years' time. You are of the new gang – the gang of virtue. The same people who sent him specially also recommended you. Oh, don't say no. I've my own eyes to trust.' Light dawned upon me. My dear aunt's influential acquaint-

ances were producing an unexpected effect upon that
young man. I nearly burst into a laugh. 'Do you read the
Company's confidential correspondence?' I asked. He
hadn't a word to say. It was great fun. 'When Mr. Kurtz,'
I continued, severely, 'is General Manager, you won't
have the opportunity.'

"He blew the candle out suddenly, and we went outside. The moon had risen. Black figures strolled about
listlessly, pouring water on the glow, whence proceeded
a sound of hissing; steam ascended in the moonlight,
the beaten nigger groaned somewhere. 'What a row the
brute makes!' said the indefatigable man with the
moustaches, appearing near us. 'Serve him right. Trans-
gression – punishment – bang! Pitiless, pitiless. That's
the only way. This will prevent all conflagrations for the
future. I was just telling the manager . . .' He noticed
my companion, and became crestfallen all at once. 'Not
in bed yet,' he said, with a kind of servile heartiness;
'it's so natural. Ha! Danger – agitation.' He vanished. I
went on to the river-side, and the other followed me. I
heard a scathing murmur at my ear, 'Heap of muffs – go
to.' The pilgrims could be seen in knots gesticulating,
discussing. Several had still their staves in their hands.
I verily believe they took these sticks to bed with them.
Beyond the fence the forest stood up spectrally in the
moonlight, and through the dim stir, through the faint
sounds of that lamentable courtyard, the silence of the
land went home to one's very heart – its mystery, its
greatness, the amazing reality of its concealed life. The
hurt nigger moaned feebly somewhere near by, and
then fetched a deep sigh that made me mend my pace
away from there. I felt a hand introducing itself under
my arm. 'My dear sir,' said the fellow, 'I don't want to
be misunderstood, and especially by you, who will
see Mr. Kurtz long before I can have that pleasure.
I wouldn't like him to get a false idea of my dis-
position . . .'

"I let him run on, this papier-maché Mephistopheles, and it seemed to me that if I tried I could poke my forefinger through him, and would find nothing inside but a little loose dirt, maybe. He, don't you see, had been planning to be assistant-manager by-and-by under the present man, and I could see that the coming of that Kurtz had upset them both not a little. He talked precipitately, and I did not try to stop him. I had my shoulders against the wreck of my steamer, hauled up on the slope like a carcass of some big river animal. The smell of mud, of primeval mud, by Jove! was in my nostrils, the high stillness of primeval forest was before my eyes; there were shiny patches on the black creek. The moon had spread over everything a thin layer of silver – over the rank grass, over the mud, upon the wall of matted vegetation standing higher than the wall of a temple, over the great river I could see through a sombre gap glittering, glittering, as it flowed broadly by without a murmur. All this was great, expectant, mute, while the man jabbered about himself. I wondered whether the stillness on the face of the immensity looking at us two were meant as an appeal or as a menace. What were we who had strayed in here? Could we handle that dumb thing, or would it handle us? I felt how big, how confoundedly big, was that thing that couldn't talk, and perhaps was deaf as well. What was in there? I could see a little ivory coming out from there, and I had heard Mr. Kurtz was in there. I had heard enough about it, too – God knows! Yet somehow it didn't bring any image with it – no more than if I had been told an angel or a fiend was in there. I believed it in the same way one of you might believe there are inhabitants in the planet Mars. I knew once a Scotch sailmaker who was certain, dead sure, there were people in Mars. If you asked him for some idea how they looked and behaved, he would get shy and mutter something about 'walking on all-fours'. If you as much as smiled, he would – though a man of sixty – offer to fight you. I would not have gone so far as to fight for Kurtz, but I went for him near enough to a lie. You know I hate, detest, and can't bear a lie, not because I am straighter than the rest of us, but simply because it appals me. There is a taint of death, a flavour of mortality in lies – which is exactly what I hate and detest in the world – what I want to forget. It makes me miserable and sick, like biting something rotten would do. Temperament, I suppose. Well, I went near enough to it by letting the young fool there believe anything he liked to imagine as to my influence in Europe. I became in an instant as much of a pretence as the rest of the bewitched pilgrims. This simply because I had a notion it somehow would be of help to that Kurtz whom at the time I did not see – you understand. He was just a word for me. I did not see the man in the name any more than you do. Do you see him? Do you see the story? Do you see anything? It seems to me I am trying to tell you a dream – making a vain attempt, because no relation of a dream can convey the dream-sensation, that commingling of absurdity, surprise, and bewilderment in a tremor of struggling revolt, that notion of being captured by the incredible which is of the very essence of dreams. . ."

He was silent for a while.

". . . No, it is impossible; it is impossible to convey the life-sensation of any given epoch of one's existence – that which makes its truth, its meaning – its subtle and penetrating essence. It is impossible. We live, as we dream – alone . . ."

He paused again as if reflecting, then added –

"Of course in this you fellows see more than I could then. You see me, whom you know . . ."

It had become so pitch dark that we listeners could hardly see one another. For a long time already he, sitting apart, had been no more to us than a voice. There was not a word from anybody. The others might have been asleep, but I was awake. I listened, I listened on the watch for the sentence, for the word, that would give me the clue to the faint uneasiness inspired by this narrative that seemed to shape itself without human lips in the heavy night-air of the river.

"... Yes – I let him run on," Marlow began again, "and think what he pleased about the powers that were behind me. I did! And there was nothing behind me! There was nothing but that wretched, old, mangled steamboat I was leaning against, while he talked fluently about 'the necessity for every man to get on'. 'And when one comes out here, you conceive, it is not to gaze at the moon.' Mr. Kurtz was a 'universal genius', but even a genius would find it easier to work with 'adequate tools – intelligent men'. He did not make bricks – why, there was a physical impossibility in the way – as I was well aware; and if he did secretarial work for the manager, it was because 'no sensible man rejects wantonly the confidence of his superiors'. Did I see it? I saw it. What more did I want? What I really wanted was rivets, by heaven! Rivets. To get on with the work – to stop the hole. Rivets I wanted. There were cases of them down at the coast – cases – piled up – burst – split! You kicked a loose rivet at every second step in that station yard on the hillside. Rivets had rolled into the grove of death. You could fill your pockets with rivets for the trouble of stooping down – and there wasn't one rivet to be found where it was wanted. We had plates that would do, but nothing to fasten them with. And every week the messenger, a lone negro, letter-bag on shoulder and staff in hand, left our station for the coast. And several times a week a coast caravan came in with trade goods – ghastly glazed calico that made you shudder only to look at it, glass beads value about a penny a quart, confounded spotted cotton handkerchiefs. And no rivets. Three carriers could have brought all that was wanted to set that steamboat afloat.

"He was becoming confidential now, but I fancy my unresponsive attitude must have exasperated him at last, for he judged it necessary to inform me he feared neither God nor devil, let alone any mere man. I said I could see that very well, but what I wanted was a certain quantity of rivets – and rivets were what really Mr. Kurtz wanted, if he had only known it. Now letters went to the coast every week . . . 'My dear sir,' he cried, 'I write from dictation.' I demanded rivets. There was a way – for an intelligent man. He changed his manner; became very cold, and suddenly began to talk about a hippopotamus; wondered whether sleeping on board the steamer (I stuck to my salvage night and day) I wasn't disturbed. There was an old hippo that had the bad habit of getting out on the bank and roaming at night over the station grounds. The pilgrims used to turn out in a body and empty every rifle they could lay hands on at him. Some even had sat up o' nights for him. All this energy was wasted, though. 'That animal has a charmed life,' he said; 'but you can say this only of brutes in this country. No man – you apprehend me? – no man here bears a charmed life.' He stood there for a moment in the moonlight with his delicate hooked nose set a little askew, and his mica eyes glittering without a wink, then, with a curt Goodnight, he strode off. I could see he was disturbed and considerably puzzled, which made me feel more hopeful than I had been for days. It was a great comfort to turn from that chap to my influential friend, the battered, twisted, ruined, tin-pot steamboat. I clambered on board. She rang under my feet like an empty Huntley & Palmer biscuit-tin kicked along a gutter; she was nothing so solid in make, and rather less pretty in shape, but I had expended enough hard work on her to make me love her. No influential friend would have served me better. She had given me a chance to come out a bit – to find out what I could do. No, I don't like work. I had rather laze about and think of all the fine

things that can be done. I don't like work – no man
does – but I like what is in the work, – the chance to
find yourself. Your own reality – for yourself, not for
others – what no other man can ever know. They can
only see the mere show, and never can tell what it really
means.

    "I was not surprised to see somebody sitting aft, on
the deck, with his legs dangling over the mud. You see
I rather chummed with the few mechanics there were
in that station, whom the other pilgrims naturally des-
pised – on account of their imperfect manners, I suppose. This was the foreman – a boiler-maker by trade –
a good worker. He was a lank, bony, yellow-faced man,
with big intense eyes. His aspect was worried, and his
head was as bald as the palm of my hand; but his hair in
falling seemed to have stuck to his chin, and had pros-
pered in the new locality, for his beard hung down to his
waist. He was a widower with six young children (he
had left them in charge of a sister of his to come out
there), and the passion of his life was pigeon-flying. He
was an enthusiast and a connoisseur. He would rave
about pigeons. After work hours he used sometimes to
come over from his hut for a talk about his children and
his pigeons; at work, when he had to crawl in the mud
under the bottom of the steamboat, he would tie up that
beard of his in a kind of white serviette he brought for
the purpose. It had loops to go over his ears. In the evening he could be seen squatted on the bank rinsing that
wrapper in the creek with great care, then spreading it
solemnly on a bush to dry.

    "I slapped him on the back and shouted 'We shall
have rivets!' He scrambled to his feet exclaiming 'No!
Rivets!' as though he couldn't believe his ears. Then in
a low voice, 'You . . . eh?' I don't know why we behaved
like lunatics. I put my finger to the side of my nose and
nodded mysteriously. 'Good for you!' he cried, snapped
his fingers above his head, lifting one foot. I tried a jig.

We capered on the iron deck. A frightful clatter came out of that hulk, and the virgin forest on the other bank of the creek sent it back in a thundering roll upon the sleeping station. It must have made some of the pilgrims sit up in their hovels. A dark figure obscured the lighted doorway of the manager's hut, vanished, then, a second or so after, the doorway itself vanished, too. We stopped, and the silence driven away by the stamping of our feet flowed back again from the recesses of the land. The great wall of vegetation, an exuberant and entangled mass of trunks, branches, leaves, boughs, festoons, motionless in the moonlight, was like a rioting invasion of soundless life, a rolling wave of plants, piled up, crested, ready to topple over the creek, to sweep every little man of us out of his little existence. And it moved not. A deadened burst of mighty splashes and snorts reached us from afar, as though an ichthyosaurus had been taking a bath of glitter in the great river. 'After all,' said the boiler-maker in a reasonable tone, 'why shouldn't we get the rivets?' Why not, indeed! I did not know of any reason why we shouldn't. 'They'll come in three weeks,' I said, confidently.

"But they didn't. Instead of rivets there came an invasion, an infliction, a visitation. It came in sections during the next three weeks, each section headed by a donkey carrying a white man in new clothes and tan shoes, bowing from that elevation right and left to the impressed pilgrims. A quarrelsome band of footsore sulky niggers trod on the heels of the donkey; a lot of tents, camp-stools, tin boxes, white cases, brown bales would be shot down in the courtyard, and the air of mystery would deepen a little over the muddle of the station. Five such instalments came, with their absurd air of disorderly flight with the loot of innumerable outfit shops and provision stores, that, one would think, they were lugging, after a raid, into the wilderness for equitable division. It was an inextricable mess of things decent in themselves but that human folly made look like spoils of thieving.

"This devoted band called itself the Eldorado Exploring Expedition, and I believe they were sworn to secrecy. Their talk, however, was the talk of sordid buccaneers: it was reckless without hardihood, greedy without audacity, and cruel without courage; there was not an atom of foresight or of serious intention in the whole batch of them, and they did not seem aware these things are wanted for the work of the world. To tear treasure out of the bowels of the land was their desire, with no more moral purpose at the back of it than there is in burglars breaking into a safe. Who paid the expenses of the noble exterprise I don't know; but the uncle of our manager was leader of that lot.

"In exterior he resembled a butcher in a poor neighbourhood, and his eyes had a look of sleepy cunning. He carried his fat paunch with ostentation on his short legs, and during the time his gang infested the station spoke to no one but his nephew. You could see these two roaming about all day long with their heads close together in an everlasting confab.

"I had given up worrying myself about the rivets. One's capacity for that kind of folly is more limited than you would suppose. I said Hang! – and let things slide. I had plenty of time for meditation, and now and then I would give some thought to Kurtz. I wasn't very interested in him. No. Still, I was curious to see whether this man, who had come out equipped with moral ideas of some sort, would climb to the top after all and how he would set about his work when there."

## II

"ONE evening as I was lying flat on the deck of my steamboat, I heard voices approaching – and there were the nephew and the uncle strolling along the bank. I laid my head on my arm again, and had nearly lost myself in a doze, when somebody said in my ear, as it were: 'I am as harmless as a little child, but I don't like to be dictated to. Am I the manager – or am I not? I was ordered to send him there. It's incredible.' . . . I became aware that the two were standing on the shore alongside the forepart of the steamboat, just below my head. I did not move; it did not occur to me to move: I was sleepy. 'It *is* unpleasant,' grunted the uncle. 'He has asked the Administration to be sent there,' said the other, 'with the idea of showing what he could do; and I was instructed accordingly. Look at the influence that man must have. Is it not frightful?' They both agreed it was frightful, then made several bizarre remarks: 'Make rain and fine weather – one man – the Council – by the nose' – bits of absurd sentences that got the better of my drowsiness, so that I had pretty near the whole of my wits about me when the uncle said, 'The climate may do away with this difficulty for you. Is he alone there?' 'Yes,' answered the manager; 'he sent his assistant down the river with a note to me in these terms: "Clear this poor devil out of the country, and don't bother sending more of that sort. I had rather be alone than have the kind of men you can dispose of with me." It was more than a year ago. Can you imagine such impudence!' 'Anything since then?' asked the other, hoarsely. 'Ivory,' jerked the nephew; 'lots of it – prime

43

sort – lots – most annoying, from him.' 'And with that?'
questioned the heavy rumble. 'Invoice,' was the reply
fired out, so to speak. Then silence. They had been
talking about Kurtz.

"I was broad awake by this time, but, lying perfectly
at ease, remained still, having no inducement to change
my position. 'How did that ivory come all this way?'
growled the elder man, who seemed very vexed. The
other explained that it had come with a fleet of canoes
in charge of an English half-caste clerk Kurtz had with
him; that Kurtz had apparently intended to return himself, the station being by that time bare of goods and
stores, but after coming three hundred miles, had suddenly decided to go back, which he started to do alone
in a small dugout with four paddlers, leaving the half-
caste to continue down the river with the ivory. The two
fellows there seemed astounded at anybody attempting
such a thing. They were at a loss for an adequate motive.
As to me, I seemed to see Kurtz for the first time. It was
a distinct glimpse: the dugout, four paddling savages,
and the lone white man turning his back suddenly on
the headquarters, on relief, on thoughts of home – perhaps; setting his face towards the depths of the wilderness, towards his empty and desolate station. I did not
know the motive. Perhaps he was just simply a fine fellow who stuck to his work for its own sake. His name,
you understand, had not been pronounced once. He was
'that man'. The half-caste, who, as far as I could see, had
conducted a difficult trip with great prudence and
pluck, was invariably alluded to as 'that scoundrel'. The
'scoundrel' had reported that the 'man' had been very
ill – had recovered imperfectly ... The two below me
moved away then a few paces, and strolled back and
forth at some little distance. I heard: 'Military post –
doctor – two hundred miles – quite alone now – unavoidable delays – nine months – no news – strange rumours.' They approached again, just as the manager was

saying, 'No one, as far as I know, unless a species of wandering trader – a pestilential fellow, snapping ivory from the natives.' Who was it they were talking about now? I gathered in snatches that this was some man supposed to be in Kurtz's district, and of whom the manager did not approve. 'We will not be free from unfair competition till one of these fellows is hanged for an example,' he said. 'Certainly,' grunted the other; 'get him hanged! Why not? Anything – anything can be done in this country. That's what I say; nobody here, you understand, *here*, can endanger your position. And why? You stand the climate – you outlast them all. The danger is in Europe; but there before I left I took care to –' They moved off and whispered, then their voices rose again. 'The extraordinary series of delays is not my fault. I did my best.' The fat man sighed. 'Very sad.' 'And the pestiferous absurdity of his talk,' continued the other; 'he bothered me enough when he was here. "Each station should be like a beacon on the road towards better things, a centre for trade of course, but also for humanizing, improving, instructing." Conceive you – that ass! And he wants to be manager! No, it's –' Here he got choked by excessive indignation, and I lifted my head the least bit. I was surprised to see how near they were – right under me. I could have spat upon their hats. They were looking on the ground, absorbed in thought. The manager was switching his leg with a slender twig: his sagacious relative lifted his head. 'You have been well since you came out this time?' he asked. The other gave a start. 'Who? I? Oh! Like a charm – like a charm. But the rest – oh, my goodness! All sick. They die so quick, too, that I haven't the time to send them out of the country – it's incredible!' 'H'm. Just so,' grunted the uncle. 'Ah! my boy, trust to this – I say, trust to this.' I saw him extend his short flipper of an arm for a gesture that took in the forest, the creek, the mud, the river, – seemed to beckon with a dishonouring flourish before

the sunlit face of the land a treacherous appeal to the
lurking death, to the hidden evil, to the profound darkness of its heart. It was so startling that I leaped to my
feet and looked back at the edge of the forest, as though
I had expected an answer of some sort to that black dis-
play of confidence. You know the foolish notions that
come to one sometimes. The high stillness confronted
these two figures with its ominous patience, waiting for
the passing away of a fantastic invasion.

"They swore aloud together – out of sheer fright, I
believe – then pretending not to know anything of my
existence, turned back to the station. The sun was low;
and leaning forward side by side, they seemed to be
tugging painfully uphill their two ridiculous shadows of
unequal length, that trailed behind them slowly over
the tall grass without bending a single blade.

"In a few days the Eldorado Expedition went into
the patient wilderness, that closed upon it as the sea
closes over a diver. Long afterwards the news came that
all the donkeys were dead. I know nothing as to the fate
of the less valuable animals. They, no doubt, like the
rest of us, found what they deserved. I did not inquire.
I was then rather excited at the prospect of meeting
Kurtz very soon. When I say very soon I mean it
comparatively. It was just two months from the day we
left the creek when we came to the bank below Kurtz's
station.

"Going up that river was like travelling back to the
earliest beginnings of the world, when vegetation rioted
on the earth and the big trees were kings. An empty
stream, a great silence, an impenetrable forest. The air
was warm, thick, heavy, sluggish. There was no joy in
the brilliance of sunshine. The long stretches of the waterway ran on, deserted, into the gloom of over-shadowed
distances. On silvery sandbanks hippos and alligators
sunned themselves side by side. The broadening waters flowed through a mob of wooded islands; you lost

your way on that river as you would in a desert, and
butted all day long against shoals, trying to find the
channel, till you thought yourself bewitched and cut off
for ever from everything you had known once – somewhere – far away – in another existence perhaps. There
were moments when one's past came back to one, as it
will sometimes when you have not a moment to spare
to yourself; but it came in the shape of an unrestful and
noisy dream, remembered with wonder amongst the
overwhelming realities of this strange world of plants,
and water, and silence. And this stillness of life did not
in the least resemble a peace. It was the stillness of an
implacable force brooding over an inscrutable intention.
It looked at you with a vengeful aspect. I got used to it
afterwards; I did not see it any more; I had no time. I
had to keep guessing at the channel; I had to discern,
mostly by inspiration, the signs of hidden banks; I
watched for sunken stones; I was learning to clap my
teeth smartly before my heart flew out, when I shaved
by a fluke some infernal sly old snag that would have
ripped the life out of the tin-pot steamboat and drowned
all the pilgrims; I had to keep a look-out for the signs
of dead wood we could cut up in the night for next
day's steaming. When you have to attend to things of
that sort, to the mere incidents of the surface, the reality
– the reality, I tell you – fades. The inner truth is hidden
– luckily, luckily. But I felt it all the same; I felt often
its mysterious stillness watching me at my monkey
tricks, just as it watches you fellows performing on your
respective tight-ropes for – what is it? half-a-crown a
tumble –"

"Try to be civil, Marlow," growled a voice, and I knew
there was at least one listener awake besides myself.

"I beg your pardon. I forgot the heartache which
makes up the rest of the price. And indeed what does
the price matter, if the trick be well done? You do your
tricks very well. And I didn't do badly either, since I

managed not to sink that steamboat on my first trip. It's a wonder to me yet. Imagine a blindfolded man set to drive a van over a bad road. I sweated and shivered over that business considerably, I can tell you. After all, for a seaman, to scrape the bottom of the thing that's supposed to float all the time under his care is the unpardonable sin. No one may know of it, but you never forget the thump – eh? A blow on the very heart. You remember it, you dream of it, you wake up at night and think of it – years after – and go hot and cold all over. I don't pretend to say that steamboat floated all the time. More than once she had to wade for a bit, with twenty cannibals splashing around and pushing. We had enlisted some of these chaps on the way for a crew. Fine fellows – cannibals – in their place. They were men one could work with, and I am grateful to them. And, after all, they did not eat each other before my face: they had brought along a provision of hippo-meat which went rotten, and made the mystery of the wilderness stink in my nostrils. Phoo! I can sniff it now. I had the manager on board and three or four pilgrims with their staves – all complete. Sometimes we came upon a station close by the bank, clinging to the skirts of the unknown, and the white men rushing out of a tumbledown hovel, with great gestures of joy and surprise and welcome, seemed very strange – had the appearance of being held there captive by a spell. The word ivory would ring in the air for a while – and on we went again into the silence, along empty reaches, round the still bends, between the high walls of our winding way, reverberating in hollow claps the ponderous beat of the stern-wheel. Trees, trees, millions of trees, massive, immense, running up high; and at their foot, hugging the bank against the stream, crept the little begrimed steamboat, like a sluggish beetle crawling on the floor of a lofty portico. It made you feel very small, very lost, and yet it was not altogether depressing, that feeling. After all, if you were small, the grimy beetle crawled on – which was just what you wanted it to do. Where the pilgrims imagined it crawled to I don't know. To some place where they expected to get something, I bet! For me it crawled towards Kurtz – exclusively; but when the steam-pipes started leaking we crawled very slow. The reaches opened before us and closed behind, as if the forest had stepped leisurely across the water to bar the way for our return. We penetrated deeper and deeper into the heart of darkness. It was very quiet there. At night sometimes the roll of drums behind the curtain of trees would run up the river and remain sustained faintly, as if hovering in the air high over our heads, till the first break of day. Whether it meant war, peace, or prayer we could not tell. The dawns were heralded by the descent of a chill stillness; the wood-cutters slept, their fires burned low; the snapping of a twig would make you start. We were wanderers on prehistoric earth, on an earth that wore the aspect of an unknown planet. We could have fancied ourselves the first of men taking possession of an accursed inheritance, to be subdued at the cost of profound anguish and of excessive toil. But suddenly, as we struggled round a bend, there would be a glimpse of rush walls, of peaked grass-roofs, a burst of yells, a whirl of black limbs, a mass of hands clapping, of feet stamping, of bodies swaying, of eyes rolling, under the droop of heavy and motionless foliage. The steamer toiled along slowly on the edge of a black and incomprehensible frenzy. The prehistoric man was cursing us, praying to us, welcoming us – who could tell? We were cut off from the comprehension of our surroundings; we glided past like phantoms, wondering and secretly appalled, as sane men would be before an enthusiastic outbreak in a madhouse. We could not understand because we were too far and could not remember, because we were travelling in the night of first ages, of those ages that are gone, leaving hardly a sign – and no memories.

"The earth seemed unearthly. We are accustomed to
look upon the shackled form of a conquered monster,
but there – there you could look at a thing monstrous
and free. It was unearthly, and the men were – No, they
were not inhuman. Well, you know, that was the worst
of it – this suspicion of their not being inhuman. It
would come slowly to one. They howled and leaped,
and spun, and made horrid faces; but what thrilled you
was just the thought of their humanity – like yours – the
thought of your remote kinship with this wild and passionate uproar. Ugly. Yes, it was ugly enough; but if you
were man enough you would admit to yourself that
there was in you just the faintest trace of a response to
the terrible frankness of that noise, a dim suspicion
of there being a meaning in it which you – you so remote
from the night of first ages – could comprehend. And
why not? The mind of man is capable of anything – because everything is in it, all the past as well as all the
future. What was there after all? Joy, fear, sorrow, devotion, valour, rage – who can tell? – but truth – truth
stripped of its cloak of time. Let the fool gape and shudder – the man knows, and can look on without a wink.
But he must at least be as much of a man as these on the
shore. He must meet that truth with his own true stuff
– with his own inborn strength. Principles won't do. Ac-
quisitions, clothes, pretty rags – rags that would fly off
at the first good shake. No; you want a deliberate belief.
An appeal to me in this fiendish row – is there? Very
well; I hear; I admit, but I have a voice, too, and for good
or evil mine is the speech that cannot be silenced. Of
course, a fool, what with sheer fright and fine sentiments, is always safe. Who's that grunting? You wonder
I didn't go ashore for a howl and a dance? Well, no – I
didn't. Fine sentiments, you say? Fine sentiments, be
hanged! I had no time. I had to mess about with white-
lead and strips of woollen blanket helping to put band-
ages on those leaky steam-pipes – I tell you. I had to

watch the steering, and circumvent those snags, and get the tin-pot along by hook or by crook. There was surface-truth enough in these things to save a wiser man. And between whiles I had to look after the savage who was fireman. He was an improved specimen; he could fire up a vertical boiler. He was there below me, and, upon my word, to look at him was as edifying as seeing a dog in a parody of breeches and a feather hat, walking on his hind-legs. A few months of training had done for that really fine chap. He squinted at the steam-gauge and at the water-gauge with an evident effort of intrepidity – and he had filed teeth, too, the poor devil, and the wool of his pate shaved into queer patterns, and three ornamental scars on each of his cheeks. He ought to have been clapping his hands and stamping his feet on the bank, instead of which he was hard at work, a thrall to strange witchcraft, full of improving knowledge. He was useful because he had been instructed; and what he knew was this – that should the water in that transparent thing disappear, the evil spirit inside the boiler would get angry through the greatness of his thirst, and take a terrible vengeance. So he sweated and fired up and watched the glass fearfully (with an impromptu charm, made of rags, tied to his arm, and a piece of polished bone, as big as a watch, stuck flatways through his lower lip), while the wooded banks slipped past us slowly, the short noise was left behind, the interminable miles of silence – and we crept on, towards Kurtz. But the snags were thick, the water was treacherous and shallow, the boiler seemed indeed to have a sulky devil in it, and thus neither that fireman nor I had any time to peer into our creepy thoughts.

"Some fifty miles below the Inner Station we came upon a hut of reeds, an inclined and melancholy pole, with the unrecognizable tatters of what had been a flag of some sort flying from it, and a neatly stacked woodpile. This was unexpected. We came to the bank, and

on the stack of firewood found a flat piece of board with
some faded pencil-writing on it. When deciphered it
said: 'Wood for you. Hurry up. Approach cautiously.'
There was a signature, but it was illegible – not Kurtz – a
much longer word. Hurry up. Where? Up the river?
'Approach cautiously.' We had not done so. But the
warning could not have been meant for the place where
it could be only found after approach. Something was
wrong above. But what – and how much? That was the
question. We commented adversely upon the imbe-
cility of that telegraphic style. The bush around said
nothing, and would not let us look very far, either. A
torn curtain of red twill hung in the doorway of the hut,
and flapped sadly in our faces. The dwelling was dismantled; but we could see a white man had lived there
not very long ago. There remained a rude table – a plank
on two posts; a heap of rubbish reposed in a dark corner,
and by the door I picked up a book. It had lost its covers,
and the pages had been thumbed into a state of extremely dirty softness; but the back had been lovingly
stitched afresh with white cotton thread, which looked
clean yet. It was an extraordinary find. Its title was, *An
Inquiry into some Points of Seamanship*, by a man Tower,
Towson – some such name – Master in his Majesty's
Navy. The matter looked dreary reading enough, with
illustrative diagrams and repulsive tables of figures, and
the copy was sixty years old. I handled this amazing an-
tiquity with the greatest possible tenderness, lest it
should dissolve in my hands. Within, Towson or Towser
was inquiring earnestly into the breaking strain of ships'
chains and tackle, and other such matters. Not a very
enthralling book; but at the first glance you could see
there a singleness of intention, an honest concern for
the right way of going to work, which made these
humble pages, thought out so many years ago, luminous
with another than a professional light. The simple old
sailor, with his talk of chains and purchases, made me

forget the jungle and the pilgrims in a delicious sensation of having come upon something unmistakably real.
Such a book being there was wonderful enough; but still
more astounding were the notes pencilled in the mar-
gin, and plainly referring to the text. I couldn't believe
my eyes! They were in cipher! Yes, it looked like cipher.
Fancy a man lugging with him a book of that description
into this nowhere and studying it – and making notes –
in cipher at that! It was an extravagant mystery.

"I had been dimly aware for some time of a worrying
noise, and when I lifted my eyes I saw the wood-pile
was gone, and the manager, aided by all the pilgrims,
was shouting at me from the river-side. I slipped the
book into my pocket. I assure you to leave off reading
was like tearing myself away from the shelter of an old
and solid friendship.

"I started the lame engine ahead. 'It must be this
miserable trader – this intruder,' exclaimed the manager, looking back malevolently at the place we had left.
'He must be English,' I said. 'It will not save him from
getting into trouble if he is not careful,' muttered the
manager darkly. I observed with assumed innocence
that no man was safe from trouble in this world.

"The current was more rapid now, the steamer
seemed at her last gasp, the stern-wheel flopped languidly, and I caught myself listening on tiptoe for the
next beat of the boat, for in sober truth I expected the
wretched thing to give up every moment. It was like
watching the last flickers of a life. But still we crawled.
Sometimes I would pick out a tree a little way ahead to
measure our progress towards Kurtz by, but I lost it invariably before we got abreast. To keep the eyes so long
on one thing was too much for human patience. The
manager displayed a beautiful resignation. I fretted and
fumed and took to arguing with myself whether or no I
would talk openly with Kurtz; but before I could come
to any conclusion it occurred to me that my speech or

my silence, indeed any action of mine, would be a mere futility. What did it matter what anyone knew or ignored? What did it matter who was manager? One gets sometimes such a flash of insight. The essentials of this affair lay deep under the surface, beyond my reach, and beyond my power of meddling.

"Towards the evening of the second day we judged ourselves about eight miles from Kurtz's station. I wanted to push on; but the manager looked grave, and told me the navigation up there was so dangerous that it would be advisable, the sun being very low already, to wait where we were till next morning. Moreover, he pointed out that if the warning to approach cautiously were to be followed, we must approach in daylight – not at dusk, or in the dark. This was sensible enough. Eight miles meant nearly three hours' steaming for us, and I could also see suspicious ripples at the upper end of the reach. Nevertheless, I was annoyed beyond expression at the delay, and most unreasonably, too, since one night more could not matter much after so many months. As we had plenty of wood, and caution was the word, I brought up in the middle of the stream. The reach was narrow, straight, with high sides like a railway cutting. The dusk came gliding into it long before the sun had set. The current ran smooth and swift, but a dumb immobility sat on the banks. The living trees, lashed together by the creepers and every living bush of the undergrowth, might have been changed into stone, even to the slenderest twig, to the lightest leaf. It was not sleep – it seemed unnatural, like a state of trance. Not the faintest sound of any kind could be heard. You looked on amazed, and began to suspect yourself of being deaf – then the night came suddenly, and struck you blind as well. About three in the morning some large fish leaped, and the loud splash made me jump as though a gun had been fired. When the sun rose there was a white fog, very warm and clammy, and more blinding than the night. It did not shift or drive; it was just there, standing all round you like something solid. At eight or nine, perhaps, it lifted as a shutter lifts. We had a glimpse of the towering multitude of trees, of the immense matted jungle, with the blazing little ball of the sun hanging over it – all perfectly still – and then the white shutter came down again, smoothly, as if sliding in greased grooves. I ordered the chain, which we had begun to heave in, to be paid out again. Before it stopped running with a muffled rattle, a cry, a very loud cry, as of infinite desolation, soared slowly in the opaque air. It ceased. A complaining clamour, modulated in savage discords, filled our ears. The sheer unexpectedness of it made my hair stir under my cap. I don't know how it struck the others: to me it seemed as though the mist itself had screamed, so suddenly, and apparently from all sides at once, did this tumultuous and mournful uproar arise. It culminated in a hurried outbreak of almost intolerably excessive shrieking, which stopped short, leaving us stiffened in a variety of silly attitudes, and obstinately listening to the nearly as appalling and excessive silence. 'Good God! What is the meaning –' stammered at my elbow one of the pilgrims, – a little fat man, with sandy hair and red whiskers, who wore side-spring boots, and pink pyjamas tucked into his socks. Two others remained open-mouthed a whole minute, then dashed into the little cabin, to rush out incontinently and stand darting scared glances, with Winchesters at 'ready' in their hands. What we could see was just the steamer we were on, her outlines blurred as though she had been on the point of dissolving, and a misty strip of water, perhaps two feet broad, around her – and that was all. The rest of the world was nowhere, as far as our eyes and ears were concerned. Just nowhere. Gone, disappeared; swept off without leaving a whisper or a shadow behind.

"I went forward, and ordered the chain to be hauled

in short, so as to be ready to trip the anchor and move
the steamboat at once if necessary. 'Will they attack?'
whispered an awed voice. 'We will be all butchered in
this fog,' murmured another. The faces twitched with
the strain, the hands trembled slightly, the eyes forgot
to wink. It was very curious to see the contrast of ex-
pressions of the white men and of the black fellows of
our crew, who were as much strangers to that part of the
river as we, though their homes were only eight hundred
miles away. The whites, of course greatly discomposed,
had besides a curious look of being painfully shocked
by such an outrageous row. The others had an alert,
naturally interested expression; but their faces were essentially quiet, even those of the one or two who
grinned as they hauled at the chain. Several exchanged
short, grunting phrases, which seemed to settle the matter to their satisfaction. Their headman, a young, broad-
chested black, severely draped in dark-blue fringed
cloths, with fierce nostrils and his hair all done up art-
fully in oily ringlets, stood near me. 'Aha!' I said, just
for good fellowship's sake. 'Catch 'im,' he snapped, with
a bloodshot widening of his eyes and a flash of sharp
teeth – 'catch 'im. Give 'im to us.' 'To you, eh?' I asked;
'what would you do with them?' 'Eat 'im!' he said, curtly, and, leaning his elbow on the rail, looked out into the
fog in a dignified and profoundly pensive attitude. I
would no doubt have been properly horrified, had it not
occurred to me that he and his chaps must be very hungry: that they must have been growing increasingly
hungry for at least this month past. They had been engaged for six months (I don't think a single one of them
had any clear idea of time, as we at the end of countless
ages have. They still belonged to the beginnings of time
– had no inherited experience to teach them as it were),
and of course, as long as there was a piece of paper written over in accordance with some farcical law or other
made down the river, it didn't enter anybody's head to

trouble how they would live. Certainly they had brought with them some rotten hippo-meat, which couldn't have lasted very long, anyway, even if the pilgrims hadn't, in the midst of a shocking hullabaloo, thrown a considerable quantity of it overboard. It looked like a high-handed proceeding; but it was really a case of legitimate self-defence. You can't breathe dead hippo waking, sleeping, and eating, and at the same time keep your precarious grip on existence. Besides that, they had given them every week three pieces of brass wire, each about nine inches long; and the theory was they were to buy their provisions with that currency in river-side villages. You can see how *that* worked. There were either no villages, or the people were hostile, or the director, who like the rest of us fed out of tins, with an occasional old he-goat thrown in, didn't want to stop the steamer for some more or less recondite reason. So, unless they swallowed the wire itself, or made loops of it to snare the fishes with, I don't see what good their extravagant salary could be to them. I must say it was paid with a regularity worthy of a large and honourable trading company. For the rest, the only thing to eat – though it didn't look eatable in the least – I saw in their possession was a few lumps of some stuff like half-cooked dough, of a dirty lavender colour, they kept wrapped in leaves, and now and then swallowed a piece of, but so small that it seemed done more for the looks of the thing than for any serious purpose of sustenance. Why in the name of all the gnawing devils of hunger they didn't go for us – they were thirty to five – and have a good tuck in for once, amazes me now when I think of it. They were big powerful men, with not much capacity to weigh the consequences, with courage, with strength, even yet, though their skins were no longer glossy and their muscles no longer hard. And I saw that something restraining, one of those human secrets that baffle probability, had come into play there. I looked at them with a swift quickening of interest – not because it occurred to me I might be eaten by them before very long, though I own to you that just then I perceived – in a new light, as it were – how unwholesome the pilgrims looked, and I hoped, yes, I positively hoped, that my aspect was not so – what shall I say? – so – unappetizing: a touch of fantastic vanity which fitted well with the dream-sensation that pervaded all my days at that time. Perhaps I had a little fever, too. One can't live with one's finger everlastingly on one's pulse. I had often 'a little fever', or a little touch of other things – the playful paw-strokes of the wilderness, the preliminary trifling before the more serious onslaught which came in due course. Yes; I looked at them as you would on any human being, with a curiosity of their impulses, motives, capacities, weaknesses, when brought to the test of an inexorable physical necessity. Restraint! What possible restraint? Was it superstition, disgust, patience, fear – or some kind of primitive honour? No fear can stand up to hunger, no patience can wear it out, disgust simply does not exist where hunger is; and as to superstition, beliefs, and what you may call principles, they are less than chaff in a breeze. Don't you know the devilry of lingering starvation, its exasperating torment, its black thoughts, its sombre and brooding ferocity? Well, I do. It takes a man all his inborn strength to fight hunger properly. It's really easier to face bereavement, dishonour, and the perdition of one's soul – than this kind of prolonged hunger. Sad, but true. And these chaps, too, had no earthly reason for any kind of scruple. Restraint! I would just as soon have expected restraint from a hyena prowling amongst the corpses of a battlefield. But there was the fact facing me – the fact dazzling, to be seen, like the foam on the depths of the sea, like a ripple on an unfathomable enigma, a mystery greater – when I thought of it – than the curious, inexplicable note of desperate grief in this savage clamour that had swept by us on the river-bank, behind the blind whiteness of the fog.

"Two pilgrims were quarrelling in hurried whispers as to which bank. 'Left.' 'No, no; how can you? Right, right, of course.' 'It is very serious,' said the manager's voice behind me; 'I would be desolated if anything should happen to Mr. Kurtz before we came up.' I looked at him, and had not the slightest doubt he was sincere. He was just the kind of man who would wish to preserve appearances. That was his restraint. But when he muttered something about going on at once, I did not even take the trouble to answer him. I knew, and he knew, that it was impossible. Were we to let go our hold of the bottom, we would be absolutely in the air – in space. We wouldn't be able to tell where we were going to – whether up or down stream, or across – till we fetched against one bank or the other – and then we wouldn't know at first which it was. Of course I made no move. I had no mind for a smash-up. You couldn't imagine a more deadly place for a shipwreck. Whether drowned at once or not, we were sure to perish speedily in one way or another. 'I authorize you to take all the risks,' he said, after a short silence. 'I refuse to take any,' I said, shortly; which was just the answer he expected, though its tone might have surprised him. 'Well, I must defer to your judgment. You are captain,' he said, with marked civility. I turned my shoulder to him in sign of my appreciation, and looked into the fog. How long would it last? It was the most hopeless look-out. The approach to this Kurtz grubbing for ivory in the wretched bush was beset by as many dangers as though he had been an enchanted princess sleeping in a fabulous castle. 'Will they attack, do you think?' asked the manager, in a confidential tone.

"I did not think they would attack, for several obvious reasons. The thick fog was one. If they left the bank in their canoes they would get lost in it, as we would be if we attempted to move. Still, I had also judged the jungle of both banks quite impenetrable – and yet eyes were in it, eyes that had seen us. The riverside bushes were certainly very thick; but the undergrowth behind was evidently penetrable. However, during the short lift I had seen no canoes anywhere in the reach – certainly not abreast of the steamer. But what made the idea of attack inconceivable to me was the nature of the noise – of the cries we had heard. They had not the fierce character boding of immediate hostile intention. Unexpected, wild, and violent as they had been, they had given me an irresistible impression of sorrow. The glimpse of the steamboat had for some reason filled those savages with unrestrained grief. The danger, if any, I expounded, was from our proximity to a great human passion let loose. Even extreme grief may ultimately vent itself in violence – but more generally takes the form of apathy . . .

"You should have seen the pilgrims stare! They had no heart to grin, or even to revile me: but I believe they thought me gone mad – with fright, maybe. I delivered a regular lecture. My dear boys, it was no good bothering. Keep a look-out? Well, you may guess I watched the fog for the signs of lifting as a cat watches a mouse; but for anything else our eyes were of no more use to us than if we had been buried miles deep in a heap of cotton-wool. It felt like it, too – choking, warm, stifling. Besides, all I said, though it sounded extravagant, was absolutely true to fact. What we afterwards alluded to as an attack was really an attempt at repulse. The action was very far from being aggressive – it was not even defensive, in the usual sense: it was undertaken under the stress of desperation, and in its essence was purely protective.

"It developed itself, I should say, two hours after the fog lifted, and its commencement was at a spot, roughly speaking, about a mile and a half below Kurtz's station. We had just floundered and flopped round a bend, when

I saw an islet, a mere grassy hummock of bright green, in the middle of the stream. It was the only thing of the kind; but as we opened the reach more, I perceived it was the head of a long sandbank, or rather of a chain of shallow patches stretching down the middle of the river. They were discoloured, just awash, and the whole lot was seen just under the water, exactly as a man's backbone is seen running down the middle of his back under the skin. Now, as far as I did see, I could go to the right or to the left of this. I didn't know either channel, of course. The banks looked pretty well alike, the depth appeared the same; but as I had been informed the station was on the west side, I naturally headed for the western passage.

"No sooner had we fairly entered it than I became aware it was much narrower than I had supposed. To the left of us there was the long uninterrupted shoal, and to the right a high, steep bank heavily overgrown with bushes. Above the bush the trees stood in serried ranks. The twigs overhung the current thickly, and from distance to distance a large limb of some tree projected rigidly over the stream. It was then well on in the afternoon, the face of the forest was gloomy, and a broad strip of shadow had already fallen on the water. In this shadow we steamed up – very slowly, as you may imagine. I steered her well inshore – the water being deepest near the bank, as the sounding-pole informed me.

"One of my hungry and forbearing friends was sounding in the bows just below me. This steamboat was exactly like a decked scow. On the deck, there were two little teak-wood houses, with doors and windows. The boiler was in the fore-end, and the machinery right astern. Over the whole there was a light roof, supported on stanchions. The funnel projected through that roof, and in front of the funnel a small cabin built of light planks served for a pilot-house. It contained a couch, two camp-stools, a loaded Martini-Henry leaning in one

corner, a tiny table, and the steering-wheel. It had a
wide door in front and a broad shutter at each side. All
these were always thrown open, of course. I spent my
days perched up there on the extreme fore-end of that
roof, before the door. At night I slept, or tried to, on the
couch. An athletic black belonging to some coast tribe,
and educated by my poor predecessor, was the helmsman. He sported a pair of brass earrings, wore a blue
cloth wrapper from the waist to the ankles, and thought
all the world of himself. He was the most unstable kind
of fool I had ever seen. He steered with no end of a
swagger while you were by; but if he lost sight of you,
he became instantly the prey of an abject funk, and
would let that cripple of a steamboat get the upper hand
of him in a minute.

"I was looking down at the sounding-pole, and feeling much annoyed to see at each try a little more of it
stick out of that river, when I saw my poleman give up
the business suddenly, and stretch himself flat on the
deck, without even taking the trouble to haul his pole
in. He kept hold on it though, and it trailed in the water.
At the same time the fireman, whom I could also see
below me, sat down abruptly before his furnace and
ducked his head. I was amazed. Then I had to look at
the river mighty quick, because there was a snag in the
fairway. Sticks, little sticks, were flying about – thick:
they were whizzing before my nose, dropping below
me, striking behind me against my pilot-house. All this
time the river, the shore, the woods, were very quiet –
perfectly quiet. I could only hear the heavy splashing
thump of the stern-wheel and the patter of these things.
We cleared the snag clumsily. Arrows, by Jove! We were
being shot at! I stepped in quickly to close the shutter
on the land-side. That fool-helmsman, his hands on the
spokes, was lifting his knees high, stamping his feet,
champing his mouth, like a reined-in horse. Confound
him! And we were staggering within ten feet of the

bank. I had to lean right out to swing the heavy shutter, and I saw a face amongst the leaves on the level with my own, looking at me very fierce and steady; and then suddenly, as though a veil had been removed from my eyes, I made out, deep in the tangled gloom, naked breasts, arms, legs, glaring eyes, – the bush was swarming with human limbs in movement, glistening, of bronze colour. The twigs shook, swayed, and rustled, the arrows flew out of them, and then the shutter came to. 'Steer her straight,' I said to the helmsman. He held his head rigid, face forward; but his eyes rolled, he kept on, lifting and setting down his feet gently, his mouth foamed a little. 'Keep quiet!' I said in a fury. I might just as well have ordered a tree not to sway in the wind. I darted out. Below me there was a great scuffle of feet on the iron deck; confused exclamations; a voice screamed, 'Can you turn back?' I caught sight of a V-shaped ripple on the water ahead. What? Another snag! A fusillade burst out under my feet. The pilgrims had opened with their Winchesters, and were simply squirting lead into that bush. A deuce of a lot of smoke came up and drove slowly forward. I swore at it. Now I couldn't see the ripple or the snag either. I stood in the doorway, peering, and the arrows came in swarms. They might have been poisoned, but they looked as though they wouldn't kill a cat. The bush began to howl. Our wood-cutters raised a warlike whoop; the report of a rifle just at my back deafened me. I glanced over my shoulder, and the pilot-house was yet full of noise and smoke when I made a dash at the wheel. The fool-nigger had dropped everything, to throw the shutter open and let off that Martini-Henry. He stood before the wide opening, glaring, and I yelled at him to come back, while I straightened the sudden twist out of that steamboat. There was no room to turn even if I had wanted to, the snag was somewhere very near ahead in that confounded smoke, there was no time to lose, so I just crowded her into the bank – right into the bank, where I knew the water was deep.

"We tore slowly along the overhanging bushes in a whirl of broken twigs and flying leaves. The fusillade below stopped short, as I had foreseen it would when the squirts got empty. I threw my head back to a glinting whizz that traversed the pilot-house, in at one shutter-hole and out at the other. Looking past that mad helmsman, who was shaking the empty rifle and yelling at the shore, I saw vague forms of men running bent double, leaping, gliding, distinct, incomplete, evanescent. Something big appeared in the air before the shutter, the rifle went overboard, and the man stepped back swiftly, looked at me over his shoulder in an extraordinary, profound, familiar manner, and fell upon my feet. The side of his head hit the wheel twice, and the end of what appeared a long cane clattered round and knocked over a little camp-stool. It looked as though after wrenching that thing from somebody ashore he had lost his balance in the effort. The thin smoke had blown away, we were clear of the snag, and looking ahead I could see that in another hundred yards or so I would be free to sheer off, away from the bank; but my feet felt so very warm and wet that I had to look down. The man had rolled on his back and stared straight up at me; both his hands clutched that cane. It was the shaft of a spear that, either thrown or lunged through the opening, had caught him in the side just below the ribs; the blade had gone in out of sight, after making a frightful gash; my shoes were full; a pool of blood lay very still, gleaming dark-red under the wheel; his eyes shone with an amazing lustre. The fusillade burst out again. He looked at me anxiously, gripping the spear like something precious, with an air of being afraid I would try to take it away from him. I had to make an effort to free my eyes from his gaze and attend to the steering. With one hand I felt above my head for the line of the steam whistle, and jerked out screech after screech hurriedly. The tumult of angry and warlike yells was checked instantly, and then from the depths of the woods went out such a tremulous and prolonged wail of mournful fear and utter despair as may be imagined to follow the flight of the last hope from the earth. There was a great commotion in the bush; the shower of arrows stopped, a few dropping shots rang out sharply – then silence, in which the languid beat of the stern-wheel came plainly to my ears. I put the helm hard a-starboard at the moment when the pilgrim in pink pyjamas, very hot and agitated, appeared in the doorway. 'The manager sends me –' he began in an official tone, and stopped short. 'Good God!' he said, glaring at the wounded man.

"We two whites stood over him, and his lustrous and inquiring glance enveloped us both. I declare it looked as though he would presently put to us some question in an understandable language; but he died without uttering a sound, without moving a limb, without twitching a muscle. Only in the very last moment, as though in response to some sign we could not see, to some whisper we could not hear, he frowned heavily, and that frown gave to his black death-mask an inconceivably sombre, brooding, and menacing expression. The lustre of inquiring glance faded swiftly into vacant glassiness. 'Can you steer?' I asked the agent eagerly. He looked very dubious; but I made a grab at his arm, and he understood at once I meant him to steer whether or no. To tell you the truth, I was morbidly anxious to change my shoes and socks. 'He is dead,' murmured the fellow, immensely impressed. 'No doubt about it,' said I, tugging like mad at the shoe-laces. 'And by the way, I suppose Mr. Kurtz is dead as well by this time.'

"For the moment that was the dominant thought. There was a sense of extreme disappointment, as though I had found out I had been striving after something altogether without a substance. I couldn't have been more disgusted if I had travelled all this way for the sole purpose of talking with Mr. Kurtz. Talking with ... I flung one shoe overboard, and became aware that that was exactly what I had been looking forward to – a talk with Kurtz. I made the strange discovery that I had never imagined him as doing, you know, but as discoursing. I didn't say to myself, 'Now I will never see him,' or 'Now I will never shake him by the hand,' but, 'Now I will never hear him.' The man presented himself as a voice. Not of course that I did not connect him with some sort of action. Hadn't I been told in all the tones of jealousy and admiration that he had collected, bartered, swindled, or stolen more ivory than all the other agents together? That was not the point. The point was in his being a gifted creature, and that of all his gifts the one that stood out pre-eminently, that carried with it a sense of real presence, was his ability to talk, his words – the gift of expression, the bewildering, the illuminating, the most exalted and the most contemptible, the pulsating stream of light, or the deceitful flow from the heart of an impenetrable darkness.

"The other shoe went flying unto the devil-god of that river. I thought, By Jove! it's all over. We are too late; he has vanished – the gift has vanished, by means of some spear, arrow, or club. I will never hear that chap speak after all, – and my sorrow had a startling extravagance of emotion, even such as I had noticed in the howling sorrow of these savages in the bush. I couldn't have felt more of lonely desolation somehow, had I been robbed of a belief or had missed my destiny in life... Why do you sigh in this beastly way, somebody? Absurd? Well, absurd. Good Lord! mustn't a man ever – Here, give me some tobacco." ...

There was a pause of profound stillness, then a match flared, and Marlow's lean face appeared, worn, hollow, with downward folds and dropped eyelids, with an aspect of concentrated attention; and as he took vigorous draws at his pipe, it seemed to retreat and advance out of the night in the regular flicker of the tiny flame. The match went out.

"Absurd!" he cried. "This is the worst of trying to tell. . . Here you all are, each moored with two good addresses, like a hulk with two anchors, a butcher round one corner, a policeman round another, excellent appetites, and temperature normal – you hear – normal from year's end to year's end. And you say, Absurd! Absurd be – exploded! Absurd! My dear boys, what can you expect from a man who out of sheer nervousness had just flung overboard a pair of new shoes! Now I think of it, it is amazing I did not shed tears. I am, upon the whole, proud of my fortitude. I was cut to the quick at the idea of having lost the inestimable privilege of listening to the gifted Kurtz. Of course I was wrong. The privilege was waiting for me. Oh, yes, I heard more than enough. And I was right, too. A voice. He was very little more than a voice. And I heard – him – it – this voice – other voices – all of them were so little more than voices – and the memory of that time itself lingers around me, impalpable, like a dying vibration of one immense jabber, silly, atrocious, sordid, savage, or simply mean, without any kind of sense. Voices, voices – even the girl herself – now –"

He was silent for a long time.

"I laid the ghost of his gifts at last with a lie," he began, suddenly. "Girl! What? Did I mention a girl? Oh, she is out of it – completely. They – the women I mean – are out of it – should be out of it. We must help them to stay in that beautiful world of their own, lest ours gets worse. Oh, she had to be out of it. You should have heard the disinterred body of Mr. Kurtz saying, 'My Intended.' You would have perceived directly then how completely she was out of it. And the lofty frontal bone of Mr. Kurtz! They say the hair goes on growing sometimes, but this – ah – specimen, was impressively bald.

The wilderness had patted him on the head, and, behold, it was like a ball – an ivory ball; it had caressed him,
and – lo! – he had withered; it had taken him, loved
him, embraced him, got into his veins, consumed his
flesh, and sealed his soul to its own by the inconceivable
ceremonies of some devilish initiation. He was its
spoiled and pampered favourite. Ivory? I should think
so. Heaps of it, stacks of it. The old mud shanty was
bursting with it. You would think there was not a single
tusk left either above or below the ground in the whole
country. 'Mostly fossil,' the manager had remarked, dis-
paragingly. It was no more fossil than I am; but they call
it fossil when it is dug up. It appears these niggers
do bury the tusks sometimes – but evidently they
couldn't bury this parcel deep enough to save the gifted
Mr. Kurtz from his fate. We filled the steamboat with it,
and had to pile a lot on the deck. Thus he could see and
enjoy as long as he could see, because the appreciation
of this favour had remained with him to the last. You
should have heard him say, 'My ivory.' Oh yes, I heard
him. 'My Intended, my ivory, my station, my river, my –'
everything belonged to him. It made me hold my
breath in expectation of hearing the wilderness burst
into a prodigious peal of laughter that would shake the
fixed stars in their places. Everything belonged to him
– but that was a trifle. The thing was to know what he
belonged to, how many powers of darkness claimed him
for their own. That was the reflection that made you
creepy all over. It was impossible – it was not good for
one either – trying to imagine. He had taken a high seat
amongst the devils of the land – I mean literally. You
can't understand. How could you? – with solid pave-
ment under your feet, surrounded by kind neighbours
ready to cheer you or to fall on you, stepping delicately
between the butcher and the policeman, in the holy terror of scandal and gallows and lunatic asylums – how can
you imagine what particular region of the first ages a

man's untrammelled feet may take him into by the way
of solitude – utter solitude without a policeman – by the
way of silence – utter silence, where no warning voice
of a kind neighbour can be heard whispering of public
opinion? These little things make all the great difference. When they are gone you must fall back upon
your own innate strength, upon your own capacity for
faithfulness. Of course you may be too much of a fool to
go wrong – too dull even to know you are being as-
saulted by the powers of darkness. I take it, no fool ever
made a bargain for his soul with the devil: the fool is too
much of a fool, or the devil too much of a devil – I don't
know which. Or you may be such a thunderingly exalted
creature as to be altogether deaf and blind to anything
but heavenly sights and sounds. Then the earth for you
is only a standing place – and whether to be like this is
your loss or your gain I won't pretend to say. But most
of us are neither one nor the other. The earth for us is a
place to live in, where we must put up with sights, with
sounds, with smells, too, by Jove! – breathe dead hippo,
so to speak, and not be contaminated. And there, don't
you see? your strength comes in, the faith in your ability
for the digging of unostentatious holes to bury the stuff
in – your power of devotion, not to yourself, but to an
obscure, back-breaking business. And that's difficult
enough. Mind, I am not trying to excuse or even explain
– I am trying to account to myself for – for – Mr. Kurtz
– for the shade of Mr. Kurtz. This initiated wraith from
the back of Nowhere honoured me with its amazing
confidence before it vanished altogether. This was because it could speak English to me. The original Kurtz
had been educated partly in England, and – as he was
good enough to say himself – his sympathies were in the
right place. His mother was half-English, his father was
half-French. All Europe contributed to the making of
Kurtz; and by-and-by I learned that, most appropriately,
the International Society for the Suppression of Savage

Customs had entrusted him with the making of a report, for its future guidance. And he had written it, too. I've seen it. I've read it. It was eloquent, vibrating with eloquence, but too high-strung, I think. Seventeen pages of close writing he had found time for! But this must have been before his – let us say – nerves, went wrong, and caused him to preside at certain midnight dances ending with unspeakable rites, which – as far as I reluctantly gathered from what I heard at various times – were offered up to him – do you understand? – to Mr. Kurtz himself. But it was a beautiful piece of writing. The opening paragraph, however, in the light of later information, strikes me now as ominous. He began with the argument that we whites, from the point of development we had arrived at, 'must necessarily appear to them [savages] in the nature of supernatural beings – we approach them with the might as of a deity', and so on, and so on. 'By the simple exercise of our will we can exert a power for good practically unbounded,' etc. etc. From that point he soared and took me with him. The peroration was magnificent, though difficult to remember, you know. It gave me the notion of an exotic Immensity ruled by an august Benevolence. It made me tingle with enthusiasm. This was the unbounded power of eloquence – of words – of burning noble words. There were no practical hints to interrupt the magic current of phrases, unless a kind of note at the foot of the last page, scrawled evidently much later, in an unsteady hand, may be regarded as the exposition of a method. It was very simple, and at the end of that moving appeal to every altruistic sentiment it blazed at you, luminous and terrifying, like a flash of lightning in a serene sky: 'Exterminate all the brutes!' The curious part was that he had apparently forgotten all about that valuable postscriptum, because, later on, when he in a sense came to himself, he repeatedly entreated me to take good care of 'my pamphlet' (he called it), as it was sure to have in the future a good influence upon his career. I had full information about all these things, and, besides, as it turned out, I was to have the care of his memory. I've done enough for it to give me the indisputable right to lay it, if I choose, for an everlasting rest in the dust-bin of progress, amongst all the sweepings and, figuratively speaking, all the dead cats of civilization. But then, you see, I can't choose. He won't be forgotten. Whatever he was, he was not common. He had the power to charm or frighten rudimentary souls into an aggravated witch-dance in his honour; he could also fill the small souls of the pilgrims with bitter misgivings: he had one devoted friend at least, and he had conquered one soul in the world that was neither rudimentary nor tainted with self-seeking. No; I can't forget him, though I am not prepared to affirm the fellow was exactly worth the life we lost in getting to him. I missed my late helmsman awfully, – I missed him even while his body was still lying in the pilot-house. Perhaps you will think it passing strange this regret for a savage who was of no more account than a grain of sand in a black Sahara. Well, don't you see, he had done something, he had steered; for months I had him at my back – a help – an instrument. It was a kind of partnership. He steered for me – I had to look after him, I worried about his deficiencies, and thus a subtle bond had been created, of which I only became aware when it was suddenly broken. And the intimate profundity of that look he gave me when he received his hurt remains to this day in my memory – like a claim of distant kinship affirmed in a supreme moment.

"Poor fool! If he had only left that shutter alone. He had no restraint, no restraint – just like Kurtz – a tree swayed by the wind. As soon as I had put on a dry pair of slippers, I dragged him out, after first jerking the spear out of his side, which operation I confess I performed with my eyes shut tight. His heels leaped

together over the little door-step; his shoulders were
pressed to my breast; I hugged him from behind des-
perately. Oh! he was heavy, heavy; heavier than any man
on earth, I should imagine. Then without more ado I
tipped him overboard. The current snatched him as
though he had been a wisp of grass, and I saw the body
roll over twice before I lost sight of it for ever. All the
pilgrims and the manager were then congregated on the
awning-deck about the pilot-house, chattering at each
other like a flock of excited magpies, and there was a
scandalized murmur at my heartless promptitude. What
they wanted to keep that body hanging about for I can't
guess. Embalm it, maybe. But I had also heard another,
and a very ominous, murmur on the deck below. My
friends the wood-cutters were likewise scandalized, and
with a better show of reason – though I admit that the
reason itself was quite inadmissible. Oh, quite! I had
made up my mind that if my late helmsman was to be
eaten, the fishes alone should have him. He had been a
very second-rate helmsman while alive, but now he was
dead he might have become a first-class temptation, and
possibly cause some startling trouble. Besides, I was
anxious to take the wheel, the man in pink pyjamas
showing himself a hopeless duffer at the business.

"This I did directly the simple funeral was over. We
were going half-speed, keeping right in the middle of
the stream, and I listened to the talk about me. They
had given up Kurtz, they had given up the station; Kurtz
was dead, and the station had been burnt – and so on –
and so on. The red-haired pilgrim was beside himself
with the thought that at least this poor Kurtz had been
properly avenged. 'Say! We must have made a glorious
slaughter of them in the bush. Eh? What do you think?
Say?' He positively danced, the bloodthirsty little
gingery beggar. And he had nearly fainted when he saw
the wounded man! I could not help saying, 'You made a
glorious lot of smoke, anyhow.' I had seen, from the way

the tops of the bushes rustled and flew, that almost all the shots had gone too high. You can't hit anything unless you take aim and fire from the shoulder; but these chaps fired from the hip with their eyes shut. The retreat, I maintained – and I was right – was caused by the screeching of the steam-whistle. Upon this they forgot Kurtz, and began to howl at me with indignant protests.

"The manager stood by the wheel murmuring confidentially about the necessity of getting well away down the river before dark at all events, when I saw in the distance a clearing on the river-side and the outlines of some sort of building. 'What's this?' I asked. He clapped his hands in wonder. 'The station!' he cried. I edged in at once, still going half-speed.

"Through my glasses I saw the slope of a hill interspersed with rare trees and perfectly free from undergrowth. A long decaying building on the summit was half buried in the high grass; the large holes in the peaked roof gaped black from afar; the jungle and the woods made a background. There was no enclosure or fence of any kind; but there had been one apparently, for near the house half-a-dozen slim posts remained in a row, roughly trimmed, and with their upper ends ornamented with round carved balls. The rails, or whatever there had been between, had disappeared. Of course the forest surrounded all that. The river-bank was clear, and on the water-side I saw a white man under a hat like a cart-wheel beckoning persistently with his whole arm. Examining the edge of the forest above and below, I was almost certain I could see movements – human forms gliding here and there. I steamed past prudently, then stopped the engines and let her drift down. The man on the shore began to shout, urging us to land. 'We have been attacked,' screamed the manager. 'I know – I know. It's all right,' yelled back the other, as cheerful as you please. 'Come along. It's all right. I am glad.'

"His aspect reminded me of something I had seen – something funny I had seen somewhere. As I man-œuvred to get alongside, I was asking myself, 'What does this fellow look like?' Suddenly I got it. He looked like a harlequin. His clothes had been made of some stuff that was brown holland probably, but it was covered with patches all over, with bright patches, blue, red, and yellow, – patches on the back, patches on the front, patches on elbows, on knees; coloured binding around his jacket, scarlet edging at the bottom of his trousers; and the sunshine made him look extremely gay and wonderfully neat withal, because you could see how beautifully all this patching had been done. A beardless, boyish face, very fair, no features to speak of, nose peeling, little blue eyes, smiles and frowns chasing each other over that open countenance like sunshine and shadow on a wind-swept plain. 'Look out, captain!' he cried; 'there's a snag lodged in here last night.' What! Another snag? I confess I swore shamefully. I had nearly holed my cripple, to finish off that charming trip. The harlequin on the bank turned his little pug-nose up to me. 'You English?' he asked, all smiles. 'Are you?' I shouted from the wheel. The smiles vanished, and he shook his head as if sorry for my disappointment. Then he brightened up. 'Never mind!' he cried, encouraging-ly. 'Are we in time?' I asked. 'He is up there,' he replied, with a toss of the head up the hill, and becoming gloomy all of a sudden. His face was like the autumn sky, over-cast one moment and bright the next.

"When the manager, escorted by the pilgrims, all of them armed to the teeth, had gone to the house this chap came on board. 'I say, I don't like this. These nat-ives are in the bush,' I said. He assured me earnestly it was all right. 'They are simple people,' he added; 'well, I am glad you came. It took me all my time to keep them off.' 'But you said it was all right,' I cried. 'Oh, they meant no harm,' he said; and as I stared he corrected himself, 'Not exactly.' Then vivaciously, 'My faith, your pilot-house wants a clean up!' In the next breath he advised me to keep enough steam on the boiler to blow the whistle in case of any trouble. 'One good screech will do more for you than all your rifles. They are simple people,' he repeated. He rattled away at such a rate he quite overwhelmed me. He seemed to be trying to make up for lots of silence, and actually hinted, laughing, that such was the case. 'Don't you talk with Mr. Kurtz?' I said. 'You don't talk with that man – you listen to him,' he exclaimed with severe exaltation. 'But now –' He waved his arm, and in the twinkling of an eye was in the uttermost depths of despondency. In a moment he came up again with a jump, possessed himself of both my hands, shook them continuously, while he gabbled: 'Brother sailor . . . honour . . . pleasure . . . delight . . . introduce myself . . . Russian . . . son of an arch-priest . . . Government of Tambov . . . What? Tobacco! English tobacco; the excellent English tobacco! Now, that's brotherly. Smoke? Where's a sailor that does not smoke?'

"The pipe soothed him, and gradually I made out he had run away from school, had gone to sea in a Russian ship; ran away again; served some time in English ships; was now reconciled with the arch-priest. He made a point of that. 'But when one is young one must see things, gather experience, ideas; enlarge the mind.' 'Here!' I interrupted. 'You can never tell! Here I met Mr. Kurtz,' he said, youthfully solemn and reproachful. I held my tongue after that. It appears he had persuaded a Dutch trading-house on the coast to fit him out with stores and goods, and had started for the interior with a light heart, and no more idea of what would happen to him than a baby. He had been wandering about that river for nearly two years alone, cut off from everybody and everything. 'I am not so young as I look. I am twenty-five,' he said. 'At first old Van Shuyten would tell me to go to the devil,' he narrated with keen enjoyment; 'but I stuck to him, and talked and talked, till at last he got afraid I would talk the hind-leg off his favourite dog, so he gave me some cheap things and a few guns, and told me he hoped he would never see my face again. Good old Dutchman, Van Shuyten. I've sent him one small lot of ivory a year ago, so that he can't call me a little thief when I get back. I hope he got it. And for the rest I don't care. I had some wood stacked for you. That was my old house. Did you see?'

"I gave him Towson's book. He made as though he would kiss me, but restrained himself. 'The only book I had left, and I thought I had lost it,' he said, looking at it ecstatically. 'So many accidents happen to a man going about alone, you know. Canoes get upset sometimes – and sometimes you've got to clear out so quick when the people get angry.' He thumbed the pages. 'You made notes in Russian?' I asked. He nodded. 'I thought they were written in cipher,' I said. He laughed, then became serious. 'I had lots of trouble to keep these people off,' he said. 'Did they want to kill you?' I asked. 'Oh, no!' he cried, and checked himself. 'Why did they attack us?' I pursued. He hesitated, then said shamefacedly, 'They don't want him to go.' 'Don't they?' I said, curiously. He nodded a nod full of mystery and wisdom. 'I tell you,' he cried, 'this man has enlarged my mind.' He opened his arms wide, staring at me with his little blue eyes that were perfectly round."

## III

" I LOOKED at him, lost in astonishment. There he was
before me, in motley, as though he had absconded
from a troupe of mimes, enthusiastic, fabulous. His
very existence was improbable, inexplicable, and altogether bewildering. He was an insoluble problem. It
was inconceivable how he had existed, how he had suc-
ceeded in getting so far, how he had managed to remain
– why he did not instantly disappear. 'I went a little
farther,' he said, 'then still a little farther – till I had gone
so far that I don't know how I'll ever get back. Never
mind. Plenty time. I can manage. You take Kurtz away
quick – quick – I tell you.' The glamour of youth enveloped his particoloured rags, his destitution, his
loneliness, the essential desolation of his futile wander-
ings. For months – for years – his life hadn't been worth
a day's purchase; and there he was gallantly, thought-
lessly alive, to all appearance indestructible solely by
the virtue of his few years and of his unreflecting audacity. I was seduced into something like admiration – like
envy. Glamour urged him on, glamour kept him un-
scathed. He surely wanted nothing from the wilderness
but space to breathe in and to push on through. His need
was to exist, and to move onwards at the greatest
possible risk, and with a maximum of privation. If the
absolutely pure, uncalculating, unpractical spirit of adventure had ever ruled a human being, it ruled this be-
patched youth. I almost envied him the possession of
this modest and clear flame. It seemed to have consumed all thought of self so completely, that even while
he was talking to you, you forgot that it was he – the man

before your eyes – who had gone through these things. I did not envy him his devotion to Kurtz, though. He had not meditated over it. It came to him, and he accepted it with a sort of eager fatalism. I must say that to me it appeared about the most dangerous thing in every way he had come upon so far.

"They had come together unavoidably, like two ships becalmed near each other, and lay rubbing sides at last. I suppose Kurtz wanted an audience, because on a certain occasion, when encamped in the forest, they had talked all night, or more probably Kurtz had talked. 'We talked of everything,' he said, quite transported at the recollection. 'I forgot there was such a thing as sleep. The night did not seem to last an hour. Everything! Everything! . . . Of love, too.' 'Ah, he talked to you of love!' I said, much amused. 'It isn't what you think,' he cried, almost passionately. 'It was in general. He made me see things – things.'

"He threw his arms up. We were on deck at the time, and the headman of my wood-cutters, lounging near by, turned upon him his heavy and glittering eyes. I looked around, and I don't know why, but I assure you that never, never before, did this land, this river, this jungle, the very arch of this blazing sky, appear to me so hopeless and so dark, so impenetrable to human thought, so pitiless to human weakness. 'And, ever since, you have been with him, of course?' I said.

"On the contrary. It appears their intercourse had been very much broken by various causes. He had, as he informed me proudly, managed to nurse Kurtz through two illnesses (he alluded to it as you would to some risky feat), but as a rule Kurtz wandered alone, far in the depths of the forest. 'Very often coming to this station, I had to wait days and days before he would turn up,' he said. 'Ah, it was worth waiting for! – sometimes.' 'What was he doing? exploring or what?' I asked. 'Oh, yes, of course'; he had discovered lots of villages, a lake, too – he did not know exactly in what direction; it was dangerous to inquire too much – but mostly his expeditions had been for ivory. 'But he had no goods to trade with by that time,' I objected. 'There's a good lot of cartridges left even yet,' he answered, looking away. 'To speak plainly, he raided the country,' I said. He nodded. 'Not alone, surely!' He muttered something about the villages round that lake. 'Kurtz got the tribe to follow him, did he?' I suggested. He fidgeted a little. 'They adored him,' he said. The tone of these words was so extraordinary that I looked at him searchingly. It was curious to see his mingled eagerness and reluctance to speak of Kurtz. The man filled his life, occupied his thoughts, swayed his emotions. 'What can you expect?' he burst out; 'he came to them with thunder and lightning, you know – and they had never seen anything like it – and very terrible. He could be very terrible. You can't judge Mr. Kurtz as you would an ordinary man. No, no, no! Now – just to give you an idea – I don't mind telling you, he wanted to shoot me, too, one day – but I don't judge him.' 'Shoot you!' I cried. 'What for?' 'Well, I had a small lot of ivory the chief of that village near my house gave me. You see I used to shoot game for them. Well, he wanted it, and wouldn't hear reason. He declared he would shoot me unless I gave him the ivory and then cleared out of the country, because he could do so, and had a fancy for it, and there was nothing on earth to prevent him killing whom he jolly well pleased. And it was true, too. I gave him the ivory. What did I care! But I didn't clear out. No, no. I couldn't leave him. I had to be careful, of course, till we got friendly again for a time. He had his second illness then. Afterwards I had to keep out of the way; but I didn't mind. He was living for the most part in those villages on the lake. When he came down to the river, sometimes he would take to me, and sometimes it was better for me to be careful. This man suffered too much. He hated all this, and somehow he couldn't get away. When I had a chance I begged him to try and leave while there was time; I offered to go back with him. And he would say yes, and then he would remain; go off on another ivory hunt; disappear for weeks; forget himself amongst these people – forget himself – you know.' 'Why! he's mad,' I said. He protested indignantly. Mr. Kurtz couldn't be mad. If I had heard him talk, only two days ago, I wouldn't dare hint at such a thing. . . I had taken up my binoculars while we talked, and was looking at the shore, sweeping the limit of the forest at each side and at the back of the house. The consciousness of there being people in that bush, so silent, so quiet – as silent and quiet as the ruined house on the hill – made me uneasy. There was no sign on the face of nature of this amazing tale that was not so much told as suggested to me in desolate exclamations, completed by shrugs, in interrupted phrases, in hints ending in deep sighs. The woods were unmoved, like a mask – heavy, like the closed door of a prison – they looked with their air of hidden knowledge, of patient expectation, of unapproachable silence. The Russian was explaining to me that it was only lately that Mr. Kurtz had come down to the river, bringing along with him all the fighting men of that lake tribe. He had been absent for several months – getting himself adored, I suppose – and had come down unexpectedly, with the intention to all appearance of making a raid either across the river or down stream. Evidently the appetite for more ivory had got the better of the – what shall I say? – less material aspirations. However he had got much worse suddenly. 'I heard he was lying helpless, and so I came up – took my chance,' said the Russian. 'Oh, he is bad, very bad.' I directed my glass to the house. There were no signs of life, but there was the ruined roof, the long mud wall peeping above the grass, with three little square window-holes, no two of the same size; all this brought within reach of my hand, as it were. And then I made a brusque movement, and one of the remaining posts of that vanished fence leaped up in the field of my glass. You remember I told you I had been struck at the distance by certain attempts at ornamentation, rather remarkable in the ruinous aspect of the place. Now I had suddenly a nearer view, and its first result was to make me throw my head back as if before a blow. Then I went carefully from post to post with my glass, and I saw my mistake. These round knobs were not ornamental but symbolic; they were expressive and puzzling, striking and disturbing – food for thought and also for the vultures if there had been any looking down from the sky; but at all events for such ants as were industrious enough to ascend the pole. They would have been even more impressive, those heads on the stakes, if their faces had not been turned to the house. Only one, the first I had made out, was facing my way. I was not so shocked as you may think. The start back I had given was really nothing but a movement of surprise. I had expected to see a knob of wood there, you know. I returned deliberately to the first I had seen – and there it was, black, dried, sunken, with closed eyelids – a head that seemed to sleep at the top of that pole, and, with the shrunken dry lips showing a narrow white line of the teeth, was smiling, too, smiling continuously at some endless and jocose dream of that eternal slumber.

"I am not disclosing any trade secrets. In fact, the manager said afterwards that Mr. Kurtz's methods had ruined the district. I have no opinion on that point, but I want you clearly to understand that there was nothing exactly profitable in these heads being there. They only showed that Mr. Kurtz lacked restraint in the gratification of his various lusts, that there was something wanting in him – some small matter which, when the pressing need arose, could not be found under his magnificent eloquence. Whether he knew of this deficiency himself I can't say. I think the knowledge came to him at last – only at the very last. But the wilderness had found him out early, and had taken on him a terrible vengeance for the fantastic invasion. I think it had whispered to him things about himself which he did not know, things of which he had no conception till he took counsel with this great solitude – and the whisper had proved irresistibly fascinating. It echoed loudly within him because he was hollow at the core . . . I put down the glass, and the head that had appeared near enough to be spoken to seemed at once to have leaped away from me into inaccessible distance.

"The admirer of Mr. Kurtz was a bit crestfallen. In a hurried, indistinct voice he began to assure me he had not dared to take these – say, symbols – down. He was not afraid of the natives; they would not stir till Mr. Kurtz gave the word. His ascendancy was extraordinary. The camps of these people surrounded the place, and the chiefs came every day to see him. They would crawl . . . 'I don't want to know anything of the ceremonies used when approaching Mr. Kurtz,' I shouted. Curious, this feeling that came over me that such details would be more intolerable than those heads drying on the stakes under Mr. Kurtz's windows. After all, that was only a savage sight, while I seemed at one bound to have been transported into some lightless region of subtle horrors, where pure, uncomplicated savagery was a positive relief, being something that had a right to exist – obviously – in the sunshine. The young man looked at me with surprise. I suppose it did not occur to him that Mr. Kurtz was no idol of mine. He forgot I hadn't heard any of these splendid monologues on, what was it? on love, justice, conduct of life – or what not. If it had come to crawling before Mr. Kurtz, he crawled as much as the veriest savage of them all. I had no idea of the conditions, he said: these heads were the heads of rebels. I shocked him excessively by laughing. Rebels! What would be the next definition I was to hear? There had been enemies, criminals, workers – and these were rebels. Those rebellious heads looked very subdued to me on their sticks. 'You don't know how such a life tries a man like Kurtz,' cried Kurtz's last disciple. 'Well, and you?' I said. 'I! I! I am a simple man. I have no great thoughts. I want nothing from anybody. How can you compare me to? . . .' His feelings were too much for speech, and suddenly he broke down. 'I don't understand,' he groaned. 'I've been doing my best to keep him alive, and that's enough. I had no hand in all this. I have no abilities. There hasn't been a drop of medicine or a mouthful of invalid food for months here. He was shamefully abandoned. A man like this, with such ideas. Shamefully! Shamefully! I – I – haven't slept for the last ten nights . . .'

"His voice lost itself in the calm of the evening. The long shadows of the forest had slipped down hill while we talked, had gone far beyond the ruined hovel, beyond the symbolic row of stakes. All this was in the gloom, while we down there were yet in the sunshine, and the stretch of the river abreast of the clearing glittered in a still and dazzling splendour, with a murky and overshadowed bend above and below. Not a living soul was seen on the shore. The bushes did not rustle.

"Suddenly round the corner of the house a group of men appeared, as though they had come up from the ground. They waded waist-deep in the grass, in a compact body, bearing an improvised stretcher in their midst. Instantly, in the emptiness of the landscape, a cry arose whose shrillness pierced the still air like a sharp arrow flying straight to the very heart of the land; and, as if by enchantment, streams of human beings – of naked human beings – with spears in their hands, with bows, with shields, with wild glances and savage movements, were poured into the clearing by the dark-faced and pensive forest. The bushes shook, the grass swayed for a time, and then everything stood still in attentive immobility.

" 'Now, if he does not say the right thing to them we are all done for,' said the Russian at my elbow. The knot of men with the stretcher had stopped, too, halfway to the steamer, as if petrified. I saw the man on the stretcher sit up, lank and with an uplifted arm, above the shoulders of the bearers. 'Let us hope that the man who can talk so well of love in general will find some particular reason to spare us this time,' I said. I resented bitterly the absurd danger of our situation, as if to be at the mercy of that atrocious phantom had been a dishonouring necessity. I could not hear a sound, but through my glasses I saw the thin arm extended commandingly, the lower jaw moving, the eyes of that apparition shining darkly far in its bony head that nodded with grotesque jerks. Kurtz – Kurtz – that means short in German – don't it? Well, the name was as true as everything else in his life – and death. He looked at least seven feet long. His covering had fallen off, and his body emerged from it pitiful and appalling as from a winding-sheet. I could see the cage of his ribs all astir, the bones of his arm waving. It was as though an animated image of death carved out of old ivory had been shaking its hand with menaces at a motionless crowd of men made of dark and glittering bronze. I saw him open his mouth wide – it gave him a weirdly voracious aspect, as though he had wanted to swallow all the air, all the earth, all the men before him. A deep voice reached me faintly. He must have been shouting. He fell back suddenly. The stretcher shook as the bearers staggered forward again, and almost at the same time I noticed that the crowd of savages was vanishing without any perceptible movement of retreat, as if the forest that had ejected these beings so suddenly had drawn them in again as the breath is drawn in a long aspiration.

"Some of the pilgrims behind the stretcher carried

his arms – two shot-guns, a heavy rifle, and a light re-
volver-carbine – the thunderbolts of that pitiful Jupiter.
The manager bent over him murmuring as he walked
beside his head. They laid him down in one of the little
cabins – just a room for a bedplace and a camp-stool or
two, you know. We had brought his belated correspondence, and a lot of torn envelopes and open letters lit-
tered his bed. His hand roamed feebly amongst these
papers. I was struck by the fire of his eyes and the com-
posed languor of his expression. It was not so much the
exhaustion of disease. He did not seem in pain. This
shadow looked satiated and calm, as though for the moment it had had its fill of all the emotions.

"He rustled one of the letters, and looking straight in
my face said, 'I am glad.' Somebody had been writing
to him about me. These special recommendations were
turning up again. The volume of tone he emitted without effort, almost without the trouble of moving his lips,
amazed me. A voice! a voice! It was grave, profound,
vibrating, while the man did not seem capable of a whisper. However, he had enough strength in him – facti-
tious no doubt – to very nearly make an end of us, as
you shall hear directly.

"The manager appeared silently in the doorway; I
stepped out at once and he drew the curtain after me.
The Russian, eyed curiously by the pilgrims, was staring
at the shore. I followed the direction of his glance.

"Dark human shapes could be made out in the distance, flitting indistinctly against the gloomy border of
the forest, and near the river two bronze figures, leaning on tall spears, stood in the sunlight under fantastic
head-dresses of spotted skins, warlike and still in
statuesque repose. And from right to left along the
lighted shore moved a wild and gorgeous apparition of
a woman.

"She walked with measured steps, draped in striped
and fringed cloths, treading the earth proudly, with a

slight jingle and flash of barbarous ornaments. She carried her head high; her hair was done in the shape of a helmet; she had brass leggings to the knee, brass wire gauntlets to the elbow, a crimson spot on her tawny cheek, innumerable necklaces of glass beads on her neck; bizarre things, charms, gifts of witch-men, that hung about her, glittered and trembled at every step. She must have had the value of several elephant tusks upon her. She was savage and superb, wild-eyed and magnificent; there was something ominous and stately in her deliberate progress. And in the hush that had fallen suddenly upon the whole sorrowful land, the immense wilderness, the colossal body of the fecund and mysterious life seemed to look at her, pensive, as though it had been looking at the image of its own tenebrous and passionate soul.

"She came abreast of the steamer, stood still, and faced us. Her long shadow fell to the water's edge. Her face had a tragic and fierce aspect of wild sorrow and of dumb pain mingled with the fear of some struggling, half-shaped resolve. She stood looking at us without a stir, and like the wilderness itself, with an air of brooding over an inscrutable purpose. A whole minute passed, and then she made a step forward. There was a low jingle, a glint of yellow metal, a sway of fringed draperies, and she stopped as if her heart had failed her. The young fellow by my side growled. The pilgrims murmured at my back. She looked at us all as if her life had depended upon the unswerving steadiness of her glance. Suddenly she opened her bared arms and threw them up rigid above her head, as though in an uncontrollable desire to touch the sky, and at the same time the swift shadows darted out on the earth, swept around on the river, gathering the steamer into a shadowy embrace. A formidable silence hung over the scene.

"She turned away slowly, walked on, following the bank, and passed into the bushes to the left. Once only her eyes gleamed back at us in the dusk of the thickets before she disappeared.

" 'If she had offered to come aboard I really think I would have tried to shoot her,' said the man of patches, nervously. 'I had been risking my life every day for the last fortnight to keep her out of the house. She got in one day and kicked up a row about those miserable rags I picked up in the storeroom to mend my clothes with. I wasn't decent. At least it must have been that, for she talked like a fury to Kurtz for an hour, pointing at me now and then. I don't understand the dialect of this tribe. Luckily for me, I fancy Kurtz felt too ill that day to care, or there would have been mischief. I don't understand . . . No – it's too much for me. Ah, well, it's all over now.'

"At this moment I heard Kurtz's deep voice behind the curtain: 'Save me! – save the ivory, you mean. Don't tell me. 'Save *me*! Why, I've had to save you. You are interrupting my plans now. Sick! Sick! Not so sick as you would like to believe. Never mind. I'll carry my ideas out yet – I will return. I'll show you what can be done. You with your little peddling notions – you are interfering with me. I will return. I . . .'

"The manager came out. He did me the honour to take me under the arm and lead me aside. 'He is very low, very low,' he said. He considered it necessary to sigh, but neglected to be consistently sorrowful. 'We have done all we could for him – haven't we? But there is no disguising the fact, Mr. Kurtz has done more harm than good to the Company. He did not see the time was not ripe for vigorous action. Cautiously, cautiously – that's my principle. We must be cautious yet. The district is closed to us for a time. Deplorable! Upon the whole, the trade will suffer. I don't deny there is a remarkable quantity of ivory – mostly fossil. We must save it, at all events – but look how precarious the position is – and why? Because the method is unsound.' 'Do you,'

said I, looking at the shore, 'call it "unsound method?" '
'Without doubt,' he exclaimed, hotly. 'Don't you?' . . .
'No method at all,' I murmured after a while. 'Exactly,'
he exulted. 'I anticipated this. Shows a complete want
of judgment. It is my duty to point it out in the proper
quarter.' 'Oh,' said I, 'that fellow – what's his name? –
the brickmaker, will make a readable report for you.'
He appeared confounded for a moment. It seemed to
me I had never breathed an atmosphere so vile, and
I turned mentally to Kurtz for relief – positively for relief. 'Nevertheless I think Mr. Kurtz is a remarkable
man,' I said with emphasis. He started, dropped on me
a cold heavy glance, said very quietly, 'He *was*', and
turned his back on me. My hour of favour was over; I
found myself lumped along with Kurtz as a partisan of
methods for which the time was not ripe: I was unsound!
Ah! but it was something to have at least a choice of
nightmares.

"I had turned to the wilderness really, not to Mr.
Kurtz, who, I was ready to admit, was as good as buried.
And for a moment it seemed to me as if I also were buried in a vast grave full of unspeakable secrets. I felt an
intolerable weight oppressing my breast, the smell of
the damp earth, the unseen presence of victorious
corruption, the darkness of an impenetrable night . . .
The Russian tapped me on the shoulder. I heard him
mumbling and stammering something about 'brother
seaman – couldn't conceal – knowledge of matters that
would affect Mr. Kurtz's reputation'. I waited. For him
evidently Mr. Kurtz was not in his grave; I suspect that for
him Mr. Kurtz was one of the immortals. 'Well!' said I
at last, 'speak out. As it happens, I am Mr. Kurtz's friend
– in a way.'

"He stated with a good deal of formality that had we
not been 'of the same profession', he would have kept
the matter to himself without regard to consequences.
'He suspected there was an active ill will towards him

on the part of these white men that –' 'You are right,' I said, remembering a certain conversation I had overheard. 'The manager thinks you ought to be hanged.' He showed a concern at this intelligence which amused me at first. 'I had better get out of the way quietly,' he said, earnestly. 'I can do no more for Kurtz now, and they would soon find some excuse. What's to stop them? There's a military post three hundred miles from here.' 'Well, upon my word,' said I, 'perhaps you had better go if you have any friends amongst the savages near by.' 'Plenty,' he said. 'They are simple people – and I want nothing, you know.' He stood biting his lip, then: 'I don't want any harm to happen to these whites here, but of course I was thinking of Mr. Kurtz's reputation – but you are a brother seaman and –' 'All right,' said I, after a time. 'Mr. Kurtz's reputation is safe with me.' I did not know how truly I spoke.

"He informed me, lowering his voice, that it was Kurtz who had ordered the attack to be made on the steamer. 'He hated sometimes the idea of being taken away – and then again . . . But I don't understand these matters. I am a simple man. He thought it would scare you away – that you would give it up, thinking him dead. I could not stop him. Oh, I had an awful time of it this last month.' 'Very well,' I said. 'He is all right now.' 'Ye-e-es,' he muttered, not very convinced apparently. 'Thanks,' said I; 'I shall keep my eyes open.' 'But quiet – eh?' he urged, anxiously. 'It would be awful for his reputation if anybody here –' I promised a complete discretion with great gravity. 'I have a canoe and three black fellows waiting not very far. I am off. Could you give me a few Martini-Henry cartridges?' I could, and did, with proper secrecy. He helped himself, with a wink at me, to a handful of my tobacco. 'Between sailors – you know – good English tobacco.' At the door of the pilot-house he turned round – 'I say, haven't you a pair of shoes you could spare?' He raised one leg. 'Look.'

The soles were tied with knotted strings sandal-wise under his bare feet. I rooted out an old pair, at which he looked with admiration before tucking it under his left arm. One of his pockets (bright red) was bulging with cartridges, from the other (dark blue) peeped 'Towson's Inquiry,' etc., etc. He seemed to think himself excellently well equipped for a renewed encounter with the wilderness. 'Ah! I'll never, never meet such a man again. You ought to have heard him recite poetry – his own, too, it was, he told me. Poetry!' He rolled his eyes at the recollection of these delights. 'Oh, he enlarged my mind!' 'Goodbye,' said I. He shook hands and vanished in the night. Sometimes I ask myself whether I had ever really seen him – whether it was possible to meet such a phenomenon! . . .

"When I woke up shortly after midnight his warning came to my mind with its hint of danger that seemed, in the starred darkness, real enough to make me get up for the purpose of having a look round. On the hill a big fire burned, illuminating fitfully a crooked corner of the station-house. One of the agents with a picket of a few of our blacks, armed for the purpose, was keeping guard over the ivory; but deep within the forest, red gleams that wavered, that seemed to sink and rise from the ground amongst confused columnar shapes of intense blackness, showed the exact position of the camp where Mr. Kurtz's adorers were keeping their uneasy vigil. The monotonous beating of a big drum filled the air with muffled shocks and a lingering vibration. A steady droning sound of many men chanting each to himself some weird incantation came out from the black, flat wall of the woods as the humming of bees comes out of a hive, and had a strange narcotic effect upon my half-awake senses. I believe I dozed off leaning over the rail, till an abrupt burst of yells, an overwhelming outbreak of a pent-up and mysterious frenzy, woke me up in a bewildered wonder. It was cut short all at once, and the

low droning went on with an effect of audible and soothing silence. I glanced casually into the little cabin. A
light was burning within, but Mr. Kurtz was not there.

"I think I would have raised an outcry if I had believed my eyes. But I didn't believe them at first – the
thing seemed so impossible. The fact is I was completely unnerved by a sheer blank fright, pure abstract terror,
unconnected with any distinct shape of physical danger.
What made this emotion so overpowering was – how
shall I define it? – the moral shock I received, as if something altogether monstrous, intolerable to thought and
odious to the soul, had been thrust upon me unexpectedly. This lasted of course the merest fraction of a second, and then the usual sense of commonplace, deadly
danger, the possibility of a sudden onslaught and massacre, or something of the kind, which I saw impending,
was positively welcome and composing. It pacified me,
in fact, so much, that I did not raise an alarm.

"There was an agent buttoned up inside an ulster and
sleeping on a chair on deck within three feet of me. The
yells had not awakened him; he snored very slightly; I
left him to his slumbers and leaped ashore. I did not
betray Mr. Kurtz – it was ordered I should never betray
him – it was written I should be loyal to the nightmare
of my choice. I was anxious to deal with this shadow by
myself alone, – and to this day I don't know why I was
so jealous of sharing with anyone the peculiar blackness
of that experience.

"As soon as I got on the bank I saw a trail – a broad
trail through the grass. I remember the exultation with
which I said to myself, 'He can't walk – he is crawling
on all-fours – I've got him.' The grass was wet with dew.
I strode rapidly with clenched fists. I fancy I had some
vague notion of falling upon him and giving him a drub-
bing. I don't know. I had some imbecile thoughts. The
knitting old woman with the cat obtruded herself upon
my memory as a most improper person to be sitting at

the other end of such an affair. I saw a row of pilgrims squirting lead in the air out of Winchesters held to the hip. I thought I would never get back to the steamer, and imagined myself living alone and unarmed in the woods to an advanced age. Such silly things – you know. And I remember I confounded the beat of the drum with the beating of my heart, and was pleased at its calm regularity.

"I kept to the track though – then stopped to listen. The night was very clear; a dark blue space, sparkling with dew and starlight, in which black things stood very still. I thought I could see a kind of motion ahead of me. I was strangely cocksure of everything that night. I actually left the track and ran in a wide semicircle (I verily believe chuckling to myself) so as to get in front of that stir, of that motion I had seen – if indeed I had seen anything. I was circumventing Kurtz as though it had been a boyish game.

"I came upon him, and, if he had not heard me coming, I would have fallen over him, too, but he got up in time. He rose, unsteady, long, pale, indistinct, like a vapour exhaled by the earth, and swayed slightly, misty and silent before me; while at my back the fires loomed between the trees, and the murmur of many voices issued from the forest. I had cut him off cleverly; but when actually confronting him I seemed to come to my senses, I saw the danger in its right proportion. It was by no means over yet. Suppose he began to shout? Though he could hardly stand, there was still plenty of vigour in his voice. 'Go away – hide yourself,' he said, in that profound tone. It was very awful. I glanced back. We were within thirty yards from the nearest fire. A black figure stood up, strode on long black legs, waving long black arms, across the glow. It had horns – antelope horns, I think – on its head. Some sorcerer, some witchman, no doubt: it looked fiend-like enough. 'Do you know what you are doing?' I whispered. 'Perfectly,' he answered, raising his voice for that single word: it sounded to me far off and yet loud, like a hail through a speaking-trumpet. If he makes a row we are lost, I thought to myself. This clearly was not a case for fisticuffs, even apart from the very natural aversion I had to beat that Shadow – this wandering and tormented thing. 'You will be lost,' I said – 'utterly lost.' One gets sometimes such a flash of inspiration, you know. I did say the right thing, though indeed he could not have been more irretrievably lost than he was at this very moment, when the foundations of our intimacy were being laid – to endure – to endure – even to the end – even beyond.

" 'I had immense plans,' he muttered irresolutely. 'Yes,' said I; 'but if you try to shout I'll smash your head with –' There was not a stick or a stone near. 'I will throttle you for good,' I corrected myself. 'I was on the threshold of great things,' he pleaded, in a voice of longing, with a wistfulness of tone that made my blood run cold. 'And now for this stupid scoundrel –' 'Your success in Europe is assured in any case,' I affirmed, steadily. I did not want to have the throttling of him, you understand – and indeed it would have been very little use for any practical purpose. I tried to break the spell – the heavy, mute spell of the wilderness – that seemed to draw him to its pitiless breast by the awakening of forgotten and brutal instincts, by the memory of gratified and monstrous passions. This alone, I was convinced, had driven him out to the edge of the forest, to the bush, towards the gleam of fires, the throb of drums, the drone of weird incantations; this alone had beguiled his unlawful soul beyond the bounds of permitted aspirations. And, don't you see, the terror of the position was not in being knocked on the head – though I had a very lively sense of that danger, too – but in this, that I had to deal with a being to whom I could not appeal in the name of anything high or low. I had, even like the niggers, to invoke him – himself – his own exalted and incredible degradation. There was nothing either above or below him, and I knew it. He had kicked himself loose of the earth. Confound the man! he had kicked the very earth to pieces. He was alone, and I before him did not know whether I stood on the ground or floated in the air. I've been telling you what we said – repeating the phrases we pronounced – but what's the good? They were common everyday words – the familiar, vague sounds exchanged on every waking day of life. But what of that? They had behind them, to my mind, the terrific suggestiveness of words heard in dreams, of phrases spoken in nightmares. Soul! If anybody had ever struggled with a soul, I am the man. And I wasn't arguing with a lunatic either. Believe me or not, his intelligence was perfectly clear – concentrated, it is true, upon himself with horrible intensity, yet clear; and therein was my only chance – barring, of course, the killing him there and then, which wasn't so good, on account of unavoidable noise. But his soul was mad. Being alone in the wilderness, it had looked within itself, and, by heavens! I tell you, it had gone mad. I had – for my sins, I suppose – to go through the ordeal of looking into it myself. No eloquence could have been so withering to one's belief in mankind as his final burst of sincerity. He struggled with himself, too. I saw it, – I heard it. I saw the inconceivable mystery of a soul that knew no restraint, no faith, and no fear, yet struggling blindly with itself. I kept my head pretty well; but when I had him at last stretched on the couch, I wiped my forehead, while my legs shook under me as though I had carried half a ton on my back down that hill. And yet I had only supported him, his bony arm clasped round my neck – and he was not much heavier than a child.

"When next day we left at noon, the crowd, of whose presence behind the curtain of trees I had been acutely conscious all the time, flowed out of the woods again, filled the clearing, covered the slope with a mass of naked, breathing, quivering, bronze bodies. I steamed up a bit, then swung downstream, and two thousand eyes followed the evolutions of the splashing, thumping, fierce river-demon beating the water with its terrible tail and breathing black smoke into the air. In front of the first rank, along the river, three men, plastered with bright red earth from head to foot, strutted to and fro restlessly. When we came abreast again, they faced the river, stamped their feet, nodded their horned heads, swayed their scarlet bodies; they shook towards the fierce river-demon a bunch of black feathers, a mangy skin with a pendent tail – something that looked like a dried gourd; they shouted periodically together strings of amazing words that resembled no sounds of human language; and the deep murmurs of the crowd, interrupted suddenly, were like the responses of some satanic litany.

"We had carried Kurtz into the pilot-house: there was more air there. Lying on the couch, he stared through the open shutter. There was an eddy in the mass of human bodies, and the woman with helmeted head and tawny cheeks rushed out to the very brink of the stream. She put out her hands, shouted something, and all that wild mob took up the shout in a roaring chorus of articulated, rapid, breathless utterance.

" 'Do you understand this?' I asked.

"He kept on looking out past me with fiery, longing eyes, with a mingled expression of wistfulness and hate. He made no answer, but I saw a smile, a smile of indefinable meaning, appear on his colourless lips that a moment after twitched convulsively. 'Do I not?' he said slowly, gasping, as if the words had been torn out of him by a supernatural power.

"I pulled the string of the whistle, and I did this because I saw the pilgrims on deck getting out their rifles with an air of anticipating a jolly lark. At the sudden screech there was a movement of abject terror through that wedged mass of bodies. 'Don't! don't you frighten them away,' cried someone on deck disconsolately. I pulled the string time after time. They broke and ran, they leaped, they crouched, they swerved, they dodged the flying terror of the sound. The three red chaps had fallen flat, face down on the shore, as though they had been shot dead. Only the barbarous and superb woman did not so much as flinch, and stretched tragically her bare arms after us over the sombre and glittering river.

"And then that imbecile crowd down on the deck started their little fun, and I could see nothing more for smoke.

"The brown current ran swiftly out of the heart of darkness, bearing us down towards the sea with twice the speed of our upward progress; and Kurtz's life was running swiftly, too, ebbing, ebbing out of his heart into the sea of inexorable time. The manager was very placid, he had no vital anxieties now, he took us both in with a comprehensive and satisfied glance: the 'affair' had come off as well as could be wished. I saw the time approaching when I would be left alone of the party of 'unsound method'. The pilgrims looked upon me with disfavour. I was, so to speak, numbered with the dead. It is strange how I accepted this unforeseen partnership, this choice of nightmares forced upon me in the tenebrous land invaded by these mean and greedy phantoms.

"Kurtz discoursed. A voice! a voice! It rang deep to the very last. It survived his strength to hide in the magnificent folds of eloquence the barren darkness of his heart. Oh, he struggled! he struggled! The wastes of his weary brain were haunted by shadowy images now – images of wealth and fame revolving obsequiously round his unextinguishable gift of noble and lofty expression. My Intended, my station, my career, my ideas – these were the subjects for the occasional utterances of elevated sentiments. The shade of the original Kurtz frequented the bedside of the hollow sham, whose fate it was to be buried presently in the mould of primeval earth. But both the diabolic love and the unearthly hate of the mysteries it had penetrated fought for the possession of that soul satiated with primitive emotions, avid of lying fame, of sham distinction, of all the appearances of success and power.

"Sometimes he was contemptibly childish. He desired to have kings meet him at railway-stations on his return from some ghastly Nowhere, where he intended to accomplish great things. 'You show them you have in you something that is really profitable, and then there will be no limits to the recognition of your ability,' he would say. 'Of course you must take care of the motives – right motives – always.' The long reaches that were like one and the same reach, monotonous bends that were exactly alike, slipped past the steamer with their multitude of secular trees looking patiently after this grimy fragment of another world, the forerunner of change, of conquest, of trade, of massacres, of blessings. I looked ahead – piloting. 'Close the shutter,' said Kurtz suddenly one day; 'I can't bear to look at this.' I did so. There was a silence. 'Oh, but I will wring your heart yet!' he cried at the invisible wilderness.

"We broke down – as I had expected – and had to lie up for repairs at the head of an island. This delay was the first thing that shook Kurtz's confidence. One morning he gave me a packet of papers and a photograph – the lot tied together with a shoe-string. 'Keep this for me,' he said. 'This noxious fool' (meaning the manager) 'is capable of prying into my boxes when I am not looking.' In the afternoon I saw him. He was lying on his back with closed eyes, and I withdrew quietly, but I heard him mutter, 'Live rightly, die, die . . .' I listened. There was nothing more. Was he rehearsing some speech in his sleep, or was it a fragment of a phrase from some newspaper article? He had been writing for the papers and meant to do so again, 'for the furthering of my ideas. It's a duty.'

"His was an impenetrable darkness. I looked at him as you peer down at a man who is lying at the bottom of a precipice where the sun never shines. But I had not much time to give him, because I was helping the engine-driver to take to pieces the leaky cylinders, to straighten a bent connecting-rod, and in other such matters. I lived in an infernal mess of rust, filings, nuts, bolts, spanners, hammers, ratchet-drills – things I abominate, because I don't get on with them. I tended the little forge we fortunately had aboard; I toiled wearily in a wretched scrap-heap – unless I had the shakes too bad to stand.

"One evening coming in with a candle I was startled to hear him say a little tremulously, 'I am lying here in the dark waiting for death.' The light was within a foot of his eyes. I forced myself to murmur, 'Oh, nonsense!' and stood over him as if transfixed.

"Anything approaching the change that came over his features I have never seen before, and hope never to see again. Oh, I wasn't touched. I was fascinated. It was as though a veil had been rent. I saw on that ivory face the expression of sombre pride, of ruthless power, of craven terror – of an intense and hopeless despair. Did he live his life again in every detail of desire, temptation, and surrender during that supreme moment of complete knowledge? He cried in a whisper at some image, at some vision – he cried out twice, a cry that was no more than a breath –

" 'The horror! The horror!'

"I blew the candle out and left the cabin. The pilgrims were dining in the mess-room, and I took my place opposite the manager, who lifted his eyes to give me a questioning glance, which I successfully ignored. He leaned back, serene, with that peculiar smile of his sealing the unexpressed depths of his meanness. A continuous shower of small flies streamed upon the lamp, upon the cloth, upon our hands and faces. Suddenly the manager's boy put his insolent black head in the doorway, and said in a tone of scathing contempt –

" 'Mistah Kurtz – he dead.'

"All the pilgrims rushed out to see. I remained, and went on with my dinner. I believe I was considered brutally callous. However, I did not eat much. There was a lamp in there – light, don't you know – and outside it was so beastly, beastly dark. I went no more near the remarkable man who had pronounced a judgment upon the adventures of his soul on this earth. The voice was gone. What else had been there? But I am of course aware that next day the pilgrims buried something in a muddy hole.

"And then they very nearly buried me.

"However, as you see, I did not go to join Kurtz there and then. I did not. I remained to dream the nightmare out to the end, and to show my loyalty to Kurtz once more. Destiny. My destiny! Droll thing life is – that mysterious arrangement of merciless logic for a futile purpose. The most you can hope from it is some knowledge of yourself – that comes too late – a crop of unextinguishable regrets. I have wrestled with death. It is the most unexciting contest you can imagine. It takes place in an impalpable grayness, with nothing underfoot, with nothing around, without spectators, without clamour, without glory, without the great desire of victory, without the great fear of defeat, in a sickly atmosphere of tepid scepticism, without much belief in your own right, and still less in that of your adversary. If such is the form of ultimate wisdom, then life is a greater riddle than some of us think it to be. I was within a hair's-breadth of the last opportunity for pronouncement, and I found with humiliation that probably I would have nothing to say. This is the reason why I affirm that Kurtz was a remarkable man. He had something to say. He said it. Since I had peeped over the edge myself, I understand better the meaning of his stare, that could not see the flame of the candle, but was wide enough to embrace the whole universe, piercing enough to penetrate all the hearts that beat in the darkness. He had summed up – he had judged. 'The horror!' He was a remarkable man. After all, this was the expression of some sort of belief; it had candour, it had conviction, it had a vibrating note of revolt in its whisper, it had the appalling face of a glimpsed truth – the strange commingling of desire and hate. And it is not my own extremity I remember best – a vision of grayness without form filled with physical pain, and a careless contempt for the evanescence of all things – even of this pain itself. No! It is his extremity that I seem to have lived through. True, he had made that last stride, he had stepped over the edge, while I had been permitted to draw back my hesitating foot. And perhaps in this is the whole difference; perhaps all the wisdom, and all truth, and all sincerity, are just compressed into that inappreciable moment of time in which we step over the threshold of the invisible. Perhaps! I like to think my summing-up would not have been a word of careless contempt. Better his cry – much better. It was an affirmation, a moral victory paid for by innumerable defeats, by abominable terrors, by abominable satisfactions. But it was a victory! That is why I have remained loyal to Kurtz to the last, and even beyond, when a long time after I heard once more, not his own voice, but the echo of his magnificent eloquence thrown to me from a soul as translucently pure as a cliff of crystal.

"No, they did not bury me, though there is a period of time which I remember mistily, with a shuddering wonder, like a passage through some inconceivable world that had no hope in it and no desire. I found myself back in the sepulchral city resenting the sight of people hurrying through the streets to filch a little money from each other, to devour their infamous cookery, to gulp their unwholesome beer, to dream their insignificant and silly dreams. They trespassed upon my thoughts. They were intruders whose knowledge of life was to me an irritating pretence, because I felt so sure they could not possibly know the things I knew. Their bearing, which was simply the bearing of commonplace individuals going about their business in the assurance of perfect safety, was offensive to me like the outrageous flauntings of folly in the face of a danger it is unable to comprehend. I had no particular desire to enlighten them, but I had some difficulty in restraining myself from laughing in their faces, so full of stupid importance. I daresay I was not very well at that time. I tottered about the streets – there were various affairs to settle – grinning bitterly at perfectly respectable persons. I admit my behaviour was inexcusable, but then my temperature was seldom normal in these days. My dear aunt's endeavours to 'nurse up my strength' seemed altogether beside the mark. It was not my strength that wanted nursing, it was my imagination that wanted soothing. I kept the bundle of papers given me by Kurtz, not knowing exactly what to do with it. His mother had died lately, watched over, as I was told, by his Intended. A clean-shaved man, with an official manner and wearing gold-rimmed spectacles, called on me one day and made inquiries, at first circuitous, afterwards suavely pressing, about what he was pleased to denominate certain 'documents'. I was not surprised, because I had had two rows with the manager on the subject out there. I had refused to give up the smallest scrap out of that package, and I took the same attitude with the spectacled man. He became darkly menacing at last, and with much heat argued that the Company had the right to every bit of information about its 'territories'. And said he, 'Mr. Kurtz's knowledge of unexplored regions must have been necessarily extensive and peculiar – owing to his great abilities and to the deplorable circumstances in which he had been placed: therefore –' I assured him Mr. Kurtz's knowledge, however extensive, did not bear upon the problems of commerce or administration. He invoked then the name of science. 'It would be an incalculable loss if,' etc., etc. I offered him the report on the 'Suppression of Savage Customs', with the postscriptum torn off. He took it up eagerly, but ended by sniffing at it with an air of contempt. 'This is not what we had a right to expect,' he remarked. 'Expect nothing else,' I said. 'There are only private letters.' He withdrew upon some threat of legal proceedings, and I saw him no more; but another fellow, calling himself Kurtz's cousin, appeared two days later, and was anxious to hear all the details about his dear relative's last moments. Incidentally he gave me to understand that Kurtz had been essentially a great musician. 'There was the making of an immense success,' said the man, who was an organist, I believe, with lank gray hair flowing over a greasy coat-collar. I had no reason to doubt his statement; and to this day I am unable to say what was Kurtz's profession, whether he ever had any – which was the greatest of his talents. I had taken him for a painter who wrote for the papers, or else for a journalist who could paint – but even the cousin (who took snuff during the interview) could not tell me what he had been – exactly. He was a universal genius – on that point I agreed with the old chap, who thereupon blew his nose noisily into a large cotton handkerchief and withdrew in senile agitation, bearing off some family letters and memoranda without importance. Ultimately a journalist anxious to know something of the fate of his 'dear colleague' turned up. This visitor informed me Kurtz's proper sphere ought to have been politics 'on the popular side'. He had furry straight eyebrows, bristly hair cropped short, an eye-glass on a broad ribbon, and, becoming expansive, confessed his opinion that Kurtz really couldn't write a bit – 'but heavens! how that man could talk. He electrified large meetings. He had faith – don't you see? – he had the faith. He could get himself to believe anything – anything. He would have been a splendid leader of an extreme party.' 'What party?' I asked. 'Any party,' answered the other. 'He was an – an – extremist.' Did I not think so? I assented. Did I know, he asked, with a sudden flash of curiosity, 'what it was that had induced him to go out there?' 'Yes,' said I, and forthwith handed him the famous Report for publication, if he thought fit. He glanced through it hurriedly, mumbling all the time, judged 'it would do', and took himself off with this plunder.

"Thus I was left at last with a slim packet of letters and the girl's portrait. She struck me as beautiful – I mean she had a beautiful expression. I know that the sunlight can be made to lie, too, yet one felt that no manipulation of light and pose could have conveyed the delicate shade of truthfulness upon those features. She seemed ready to listen without mental reservation, without suspicion, without a thought for herself. I concluded I would go and give her back her portrait and those letters myself. Curiosity? Yes; and also some other feeling perhaps. All that had been Kurtz's had passed out of my hands: his soul, his body, his station, his plans, his ivory, his career. There remained only his memory and his Intended – and I wanted to give that up, too, to the past, in a way – to surrender personally all that remained of him with me to that oblivion which is the last word of our common fate. I don't defend myself. I had no clear perception of what it was I really wanted. Perhaps it was an impulse of unconscious loyalty, or the fulfilment of one of these ironic necessities that lurk in the facts of human existence. I don't know. I can't tell. But I went.

"I thought his memory was like the other memories of the dead that accumulate in every man's life – a vague impress on the brain of shadows that had fallen on it in their swift and final passage; but before the high and ponderous door, between the tall houses of a street as still and decorous as a well-kept alley in a cemetery, I had a vision of him on the stretcher, opening his mouth voraciously, as if to devour all the earth with all its mankind. He lived then before me; he lived as much as he had ever lived – a shadow insatiable of splendid appearances, of frightful realities; a shadow darker than the shadow of the night, and draped nobly in the folds of a gorgeous eloquence. The vision seemed to enter the house with me – the stretcher, the phantom-bearers, the wild crowd of obedient worshippers, the gloom of the forests, the glitter of the reach between the murky bends, the beat of the drum, regular and muffled like the beating of a heart – the heart of a conquering darkness. It was a moment of triumph for the wilderness, an invading and vengeful rush which, it seemed to me, I would have to keep back alone for the salvation of another soul. And the memory of what I had heard him say afar there, with the horned shapes stirring at my back, in the glow of fires, within the patient woods, those broken phrases came back to me, were heard again in their ominous and terrifying simplicity. I remembered his abject pleading, his abject threats, the colossal scale of his vile desires, the meanness, the torment, the tempestuous anguish of his soul. And later on I seemed to see his collected languid manner, when he said one day, 'This lot of ivory now is really mine. The Company did not pay for it. I collected it myself at a very great personal risk. I am afraid they will try to claim it as theirs though. H'm. It is a difficult case. What do you think I ought to do – resist? Eh? I want no more than justice.' . . . He wanted no more than justice – no more than justice. I rang the bell before a mahogany door on the first floor, and while I waited he seemed to stare at me out of the glassy panel – stare with that wide and immense

stare embracing, condemning, loathing all the universe.
I seemed to hear the whispered cry, 'The horror! The
horror!'

"The dusk was falling. I had to wait in a lofty drawing-room with three long windows from floor to ceiling
that were like three luminous and bedraped columns.
The bent gilt legs and backs of the furniture shone in
indistinct curves. The tall marble fireplace had a cold
and monumental whiteness. A grand piano stood mass-
ively in a corner; with dark gleams on the flat surfaces
like a sombre and polished sarcophagus. A high door
opened – closed. I rose.

"She came forward, all in black, with a pale head,
floating towards me in the dusk. She was in mourning.
It was more than a year since his death, more than a year
since the news came; she seemed as though she would
remember and mourn for ever. She took both my hands
in hers and murmured, 'I had heard you were coming.'
I noticed she was not very young – I mean not girlish.
She had a mature capacity for fidelity, for belief, for suf-
fering. The room seemed to have grown darker, as if all
the sad light of the cloudy evening had taken refuge on
her forehead. This fair hair, this pale visage, this pure
brow, seemed surrounded by an ashy halo from which
the dark eyes looked out at me. Their glance was guile-
less, profound, confident, and trustful. She carried her
sorrowful head as though she were proud of that sorrow,
as though she would say, I – I alone know how to mourn
for him as he deserves. But while we were still shaking
hands, such a look of awful desolation came upon her
face that I perceived she was one of those creatures that
are not the playthings of Time. For her he had died only
yesterday. And, by Jove! the impression was so powerful that for me, too, he seemed to have died only yesterday – nay, this very minute. I saw her and him in the
same instant of time – his death and her sorrow – I saw
her sorrow in the very moment of his death. Do you

understand? I saw them together – I heard them
together. She had said, with a deep catch of the breath,
'I have survived' while my strained ears seemed to hear
distinctly, mingled with her tone of despairing regret,
the summing-up whisper of his eternal condemnation.
I asked myself what I was doing there, with a sensation
of panic in my heart as though I had blundered into a
place of cruel and absurd mysteries not fit for a human
being to behold. She motioned me to a chair. We sat
down. I laid the packet gently on the little table, and
she put her hand over it. . . . 'You knew him well,' she
murmured, after a moment of mourning silence.

" 'Intimacy grows quickly out there,' I said. 'I knew
him as well as it is possible for one man to know
another.'

" 'And you admired him,' she said. 'It was impossible
to know him and not to admire him. Was it?'

" 'He was a remarkable man,' I said, unsteadily.
Then before the appealing fixity of her gaze, that
seemed to watch for more words on my lips, I went on,
'It was impossible not to –'

" 'Love him,' she finished eagerly, silencing me into
an appalled dumbness. 'How true! how true! But when
you think that no one knew him so well as I! I had all
his noble confidence. I knew him best.'

" 'You knew him best,' I repeated. And perhaps she
did. But with every word spoken the room was growing
darker, and only her forehead, smooth and white, remained illumined by the unextinguishable light of belief and love.

` " 'You were his friend,' she went on. 'His friend,' she
repeated, a little louder. 'You must have been, if he had
given you this, and sent you to me. I feel I can speak to
you – and oh! I must speak. I want you – you who have
heard his last words – to know I have been worthy of
him. . . It is not pride. . . Yes! I am proud to know I
understood him better than anyone on earth – he told

me so himself. And since his mother died I have had no one – no one – to – to –'

"I listened. The darkness deepened. I was not even sure whether he had given me the right bundle. I rather suspect he wanted me to take care of another batch of his papers which, after his death, I saw the manager examining under the lamp. And the girl talked, easing her pain in the certitude of my sympathy; she talked as thirsty men drink. I had heard that her engagement with Kurtz had been disapproved by her people. He wasn't rich enough or something. And indeed I don't know whether he had not been a pauper all his life. He had given me some reason to infer that it was his impatience of comparative poverty that drove him out there.

" '. . . Who was not his friend who had heard him speak once?' she was saying. 'He drew men towards him by what was best in them.' She looked at me with intensity. 'It is the gift of the great,' she went on, and the sound of her low voice seemed to have the accompaniment of all the other sounds, full of mystery, desolation, and sorrow, I had ever heard – the ripple of the river, the soughing of the trees swayed by the wind, the murmurs of the crowds, the faint ring of incomprehensible words cried from afar, the whisper of a voice speaking from beyond the threshold of an eternal darkness. 'But you have heard him! You know!' she cried.

" 'Yes, I know,' I said with something like despair in my heart, but bowing my head before the faith that was in her, before that great and saving illusion that shone with an unearthly glow in the darkness, in the triumphant darkness from which I could not have defended her – from which I could not even defend myself.

" 'What a loss to me – to us!' – she corrected herself with beautiful generosity; then added in a murmur, 'To the world.' By the last gleams of twilight I could see the glitter of her eyes, full of tears – of tears that would not fall.

" 'I have been very happy – very fortunate – very proud,' she went on. 'Too fortunate. Too happy for a little while. And now I am unhappy for – for life.'

"She stood up; her fair hair seemed to catch all the remaining light in a glimmer of gold. I rose, too.

" 'And of all this,' she went on, mournfully, 'of all his promise, and of all his greatness, of his generous mind, of his noble heart, nothing remains – nothing but a memory. You and I –'

" 'We shall always remember him,' I said, hastily.

" 'No!' she cried. 'It is impossible that all this should be lost – that such a life should be sacrificed to leave nothing – but sorrow. You know what vast plans he had. I knew of them, too – I could not perhaps understand – but others knew of them. Something must remain. His words, at least, have not died.'

" 'His words will remain,' I said.

" 'And his example,' she whispered to herself. 'Men looked up to him – his goodness shone in every act. His example –'

" 'True,' I said; 'his example, too. Yes, his example. I forgot that.'

" 'But I do not. I cannot – I cannot believe – not yet. I cannot believe that I shall never see him again, that nobody will see him again, never, never, never.'

"She put out her arms as if after a retreating figure, stretching them black and with clasped pale hands across the fading and narrow sheen of the window. Never see him! I saw him clearly enough then. I shall see this eloquent phantom as long as I live, and I shall see her, too, a tragic and familiar Shade, resembling in this gesture another one, tragic also, and bedecked with powerless charms, stretching bare brown arms over the glitter of the infernal stream, the stream of darkness. She said suddenly very low, 'He died as he lived.'

" 'His end,' said I, with dull anger stirring in me, 'was in every way worthy of his life.'

" 'And I was not with him,' she murmured. My anger subsided before a feeling of infinite pity.

" 'Everything that could be done –' I mumbled.

" 'Ah, but I believed in him more than anyone on earth – more than his own mother, more than – himself. He needed me! Me! I would have treasured every sigh, every word, every sign, every glance.'

"I felt like a chill grip on my chest. 'Don't,' I said, in a muffled voice.

" 'Forgive me. I – I – have mourned so long in silence – in silence. . . You were with him – to the last? I think of his loneliness. Nobody near to understand him as I would have understood. Perhaps no one to hear. . .'

" 'To the very end,' I said, shakily. 'I heard his very last words. . .' I stopped in a fright.

" 'Repeat them,' she murmured in a heart-broken tone. 'I want – I want – something – something – to – to live with.'

"I was on the point of crying at her, 'Don't you hear them?' The dusk was repeating them in a persistent whisper all around us, in a whisper that seemed to swell menacingly like the first whisper of a rising wind. 'The horror! the horror!'

" 'His last word – to live with,' she insisted. 'Don't you understand I loved him – I loved him – I loved him!'

"I pulled myself together and spoke slowly.

" 'The last word he pronounced was – your name.'

"I heard a light sigh and then my heart stood still, stopped dead short by an exulting and terrible cry, by the cry of inconceivable triumph and of unspeakable pain. 'I knew it – I was sure!' . . . She knew. She was sure. I heard her weeping; she had hidden her face in her hands. It seemed to me that the house would collapse before I could escape, that the heavens would fall upon my head. But nothing happened. The heavens do not fall for such a trifle. Would they have fallen, I wonder, if I had rendered Kurtz that justice which was his due? Hadn't he said he wanted only justice? But I couldn't. I could not tell her. It would have been too dark – too dark altogether. . ."

Marlow ceased, and sat apart, indistinct and silent, in the pose of a meditating Buddha. Nobody moved for a time. "We have lost the first of the ebb," said the Director, suddenly. I raised my head. The offing was barred by a black bank of clouds, and the tranquil waterway leading to the uttermost ends of the earth flowed sombre under an overcast sky – seemed to lead into the heart of an immense darkness.

# YOUTH

## A Narrative

". . . But the Dwarf answered: No; something human
is dearer to me than the wealth of all the world."
*Grimm's Tales*

# YOUTH

This could have occurred nowhere but in England, where men and sea interpenetrate, so to speak – the sea entering into the life of most men, and the men knowing something or everything about the sea, in the way of amusement, of travel, or of breadwinning.

We were sitting round a mahogany table that reflected the bottle, the claret-glasses, and our faces as we leaned on our elbows. There was a director of companies, an accountant, a lawyer, Marlow, and myself. The director had been a *Conway* boy, the accountant had served four years at sea, the lawyer – a fine crusted Tory, High Churchman, the best of old fellows, the soul of honour – had been chief officer in the P. & O. service in the good old days when mail-boats were square-rigged at least on two masts, and used to come down the China Sea before a fair monsoon with stun'-sails set alow and aloft. We all began life in the merchant service. Between the five of us there was the strong bond of the sea, and also the fellowship of the craft, which no amount of enthusiasm for yachting, cruising, and so on can give, since one is only the amusement of life and the other is life itself.

Marlow (at least I think that is how he spelt his name) told the story, or rather the chronicle, of a voyage: –

"Yes, I have seen a little of the Eastern seas; but what I remember best is my first voyage there. You fellows know there are those voyages that seem ordered for the illustration of life, that might stand for a symbol of existence. You fight, work, sweat, nearly kill yourself, sometimes do kill yourself, trying to accomplish something – and you can't. Not from any fault of yours. You simply can do nothing, neither great nor little – not a thing in the world – not even marry an old maid, or get a wretched 600-ton cargo of coal to its port of destination.

"It was altogether a memorable affair. It was my first voyage to the East, and my first voyage as second mate; it was also my skipper's first command. You'll admit it was time. He was sixty if a day; a little man, with a broad, not very straight back, with bowed shoulders and one leg more bandy than the other, he had that queer twisted-about appearance you see so often in men who work in the fields. He had a nut-cracker face – chin and nose trying to come together over a sunken mouth – and it was framed in iron-grey fluffy hair, that looked like a chin-strap of cotton-wool sprinkled with coal-dust. And he had blue eyes in that old face of his, which were amazingly like a boy's, with that candid expression some quite common men preserve to the end of their days by a rare internal gift of simplicity of heart and rectitude of soul. What induced him to accept me was a wonder. I had come out of a crack Australian clipper, where I had been third officer, and he seemed to have a prejudice against crack clippers as aristocratic and high-toned. He said to me, 'You know, in this ship you will have to work.' I said I had to work in every ship I had ever been in. 'Ah, but this is different, and you gentlemen out of them big ships; . . . but there! I daresay you will do. Join to-morrow.'

"I joined to-morrow. It was twenty-two years ago; and I was just twenty. How time passes! It was one of the happiest days of my life. Fancy! Second mate for the first time – a really responsible officer! I wouldn't have thrown up my new billet for a fortune. The mate looked me over carefully. He was also an old chap, but of another stamp. He had a Roman nose, a snow-white, long beard, and his name was Mahon, but he insisted that it should be pronounced Mann. He was well connected; yet there was something wrong with his luck, and he had never got on.

"As to the captain, he had been for years in coasters, then in the Mediterranean, and last in the West Indian trade. He had never been round the Capes. He could just write a kind of sketchy hand, and didn't care for writing at all. Both were thorough good seamen of course, and between those two old chaps I felt like a small boy between two grandfathers.

"The ship also was old. Her name was the *Judea*. Queer name, isn't it? She belonged to a man Wilmer, Wilcox – some name like that; but he has been bankrupt and dead these twenty years or more, and his name don't matter. She had been laid up in Shadwell basin for ever so long. You may imagine her state. She was all rust, dust, grime – soot aloft, dirt on deck. To me it was like coming out of a palace into a ruined cottage. She was about 400 tons, had a primitive windlass, wooden latches to the doors, not a bit of brass about her, and a big square stern. There was on it, below her name in big letters, a lot of scrollwork, with the gilt off, and some sort of a coat of arms, with the motto 'Do or Die' underneath. I remember it took my fancy immensely. There was a touch of romance in it, something that made me love the old thing – something that appealed to my youth!

"We left London in ballast – sand ballast – to load a cargo of coal in a northern port for Bankok. Bankok! I thrilled. I had been six years at sea, but had only seen Melbourne and Sydney, very good places, charming places in their way – but Bankok!

"We worked out of the Thames under canvas, with a North Sea pilot on board. His name was Jermyn, and he dodged all day long about the galley drying his handkerchief before the stove. Apparently he never slept. He was a dismal man, with a perpetual tear sparkling at the end of his nose, who either had been in trouble, or was in trouble, or expected to be in trouble – couldn't be happy unless something went wrong. He mistrusted my youth, my common-sense, and my seamanship, and made a point of showing it in a hundred little ways. I daresay he was right. It seems to me I knew very little then, and I know not much more now; but I cherish a hate for that Jermyn to this day.

"We were a week working up as far as Yarmouth Roads, and then we got into a gale – the famous October gale of twenty-two years ago. It was wind, lightning, sleet, snow, and a terrific sea. We were flying light, and you may imagine how bad it was when I tell you we had smashed bulwarks and a flooded deck. On the second night she shifted her ballast into the lee bow, and by that time we had been blown off somewhere on the Dogger Bank. There was nothing for it but go below with shovels and try to right her, and there we were in that vast hold, gloomy like a cavern, the tallow dips stuck and flickering on the beams, the gale howling above, the ship tossing about like mad on her side; there we all were, Jermyn, the captain, every one, hardly able to keep our feet, engaged on that gravedigger's work, and trying to toss shovelfuls of wet sand up to windward. At every tumble of the ship you could see vaguely in the dim light men falling down with a great flourish of shovels. One of the ship's boys (we had two), impressed by the weirdness of the scene, wept as if his heart would break. We could hear him blubbering somewhere in the shadows.

"On the third day the gale died out, and by-and-by a north-country tug picked us up. We took sixteen days in all to get from London to the Tyne! When we got into dock we had lost our turn for loading, and they hauled us off to a tier where we remained for a month. Mrs Beard (the captain's name was Beard) came from Colchester to see the old man. She lived on board. The crew of runners had left, and there remained only the officers, one boy, and the steward, a mulatto who answered to the name of Abraham. Mrs Beard was an old woman with a face all wrinkled and ruddy like a winter apple, and the figure of a young girl. She caught sight of me once, sewing on a button, and insisted on having my shirts to repair. This was something different from the captains' wives I had known on board crack clippers. When I brought her the shirts, she said: 'And the socks? They want mending, I am sure, and John's – Captain Beard's – things are all in order now. I would be glad of something to do.' Bless the old woman. She over-hauled my outfit for me, and meantime I read for the first time 'Sartor Resartus' and Burnaby's 'Ride to Khiva.' I didn't understand much of the first then; but I remember I preferred the soldier to the philosopher at the time; a preference which life has only confirmed. One was a man, and the other was either more – or less. However, they are both dead, and Mrs Beard is dead, and youth, strength, genius, thoughts, achievements, simple hearts – all dies . . . No matter.

"They loaded us at last. We shipped a crew. Eight able seamen and two boys. We hauled off one evening to the buoys at the dock-gates, ready to go out, and with a fair prospect of beginning the voyage next day. Mrs Beard was to start for home by a late train. When the ship was fast we went to tea. We sat rather silent through the meal – Mahon, the old couple, and I. I finished first, and slipped away for a smoke, my cabin being in a deck-house just against the poop. It was high water, blowing fresh with a drizzle; the double dock-gates were opened, and the steam-colliers were going in and out in the darkness with their lights burning bright, a great plashing of propellers, rattling of winches, and a lot of hailing on the pier-heads. I watched the procession of head-lights gliding high and of green lights gliding low in the night, when suddenly a red gleam flashed at me, vanished, came in to view again, and remained. The fore-end of a steamer loomed up close. I shouted down the cabin, 'Come up, quick!' and then heard a startled voice saying afar in the dark, 'Stop her, sir.' A bell jingled. Another voice cried warningly, 'We are going right into that

barque, sir.' The answer to this was a gruff 'All right,'
and the next thing was a heavy crash as the steamer
struck a glancing blow with the bluff of her bow about
our fore-rigging. There was a moment of confusion,
yelling, and running about. Steam roared. Then somebody was heard saying, 'All clear, sir.' . . . 'Are you all
right?' asked the gruff voice. I had jumped forward to
see the damage, and hailed back, 'I think so.' 'Easy astern,'
said the gruff voice. A bell jingled. 'What steamer is
that?' screamed Mahon. By that time she was no more
to us than a bulky shadow manœuvring a little way off.
They shouted at us some name – a woman's name,
Miranda or Melissa – or some such thing. 'This means
another month in this beastly hole,' said Mahon to me,
as we peered with lamps about the splintered bulwarks
and broken braces. 'But where's the captain?'

"We had not heard or seen anything of him all that
time. We went aft to look. A doleful voice arose hailing
somewhere in the middle of the dock, '*Judea* ahoy!' . . .
How the devil did he get there? . . . 'Hallo!' we shouted.
'I am adrift in our boat without oars,' he cried. A belated
waterman offered his services, and Mahon struck a
bargain with him for half-a-crown to tow our skipper
alongside; but it was Mrs Beard that came up the ladder
first. They had been floating about the dock in that
mizzly cold rain for nearly an hour. I was never so
surprised in my life.

"It appears that when he heard my shout 'Come up'
he understood at once what was the matter, caught up
his wife, ran on deck, and across, and down into our
boat, which was fast to the ladder. Not bad for a sixty-
year-old. Just imagine that old fellow saving heroically
in his arms that old woman – the woman of his life. He
set her down on a thwart, and was ready to climb back
on board when the painter came adrift somehow, and
away they went together. Of course in the confusion we
did not hear him shouting. He looked abashed. She said

cheerfully, 'I suppose it does not matter my losing the train now?' 'No, Jenny – you go below and get warm,' he growled. Then to us: 'A sailor has no business with a wife – I say. There I was, out of the ship. Well, no harm done this time. Let's go and look at what that fool of a steamer smashed.'

"It wasn't much, but it delayed us three weeks. At the end of that time, the captain being engaged with his agents, I carried Mrs Beard's bag to the railway-station and put her all comfy into a third-class carriage. She lowered the window to say, 'You are a good young man. If you see John – Captain Beard – without his muffler at night, just remind him from me to keep his throat well wrapped up.' 'Certainly, Mrs Beard,' I said. 'You are a good young man; I noticed how attentive you are to John – to Captain—' The train pulled out suddenly; I took my cap off to the old woman: I never saw her again. . . . Pass the bottle.

"We went to sea next day. When we made that start for Bankok we had been already three months out of London. We had expected to be a fortnight or so – at the outside.

"It was January, and the weather was beautiful – the beautiful sunny winter weather that has more charm than in the summertime, because it is unexpected, and crisp, and you know it won't, it can't, last long. It's like a wind-fall, like a godsend, like an unexpected piece of luck.

"It lasted all down the North Sea, all down Channel; and it lasted till we were three hundred miles or so to the westward of the Lizards: then the wind went round to the sou'west and began to pipe up. In two days it blew a gale. The *Judea*, hove to, wallowed on the Atlantic like an old candle-box. It blew day after day: it blew with spite, without interval, without mercy, without rest. The world was nothing but an immensity of great foaming waves rushing at us, under a sky low enough to touch with the hand and dirty like a smoked ceiling.

In the stormy space surrounding us there was as much flying spray as air. Day after day and night after night there was nothing round the ship but the howl of the wind, the tumult of the sea, the noise of water pouring over her deck. There was no rest for her and no rest for us. She tossed, she pitched, she stood on her head, she sat on her tail, she rolled, she groaned, and we had to hold on while on deck and cling to our bunks when below, in a constant effort of body and worry of mind.

"One night Mahon spoke through the small window of my berth. It opened right into my very bed, and I was lying there sleepless, in my boots, feeling as though I had not slept for years, and could not if I tried. He said excitedly –

"'You got the sounding-rod in here, Marlow? I can't get the pumps to suck. By God! it's no child's play.'

"I gave him the sounding-rod and lay down again, trying to think of various things – but I thought only of the pumps. When I came on deck they were still at it, and my watch relieved at the pumps. By the light of the lantern brought on deck to examine the sounding-rod I caught a glimpse of their weary, serious faces. We pumped all the four hours. We pumped all night, all day, all the week – watch and watch. She was working herself loose, and leaked badly – not enough to drown us at once, but enough to kill us with the work at the pumps. And while we pumped the ship was going from us piecemeal: the bulwarks went, the stanchions were torn out, the ventilators smashed, the cabin-door burst in. There was not a dry spot in the ship. She was being gutted bit by bit. The long-boat changed, as if by magic, into matchwood where she stood in her gripes. I had lashed her myself, and was rather proud of my handiwork, which had withstood so long the malice of the sea. And we pumped. And there was no break in the weather. The sea was white like a sheet of foam, like a caldron of boiling milk; there was not a break in the clouds, no – not the size of a man's hand – no, not for so much as ten seconds. There was for us no sky, there were for us no stars, no sun, no universe – nothing but angry clouds and an infuriated sea. We pumped watch and watch, for dear life; and it seemed to last for months, for years, for all eternity, as though we had been dead and gone to a hell for sailors. We forgot the day of the week, the name of the month, what year it was, and whether we had ever been ashore. The sails blew away, she lay broadside on under a weather-cloth, the ocean poured over her, and we did not care. We turned those handles, and had the eyes of idiots. As soon as we had crawled on deck I used to take a round turn with a rope about the men, the pumps, and the mainmast, and we turned, we turned incessantly, with the water to our waists, to our necks, over our heads. It was all one. We had forgotten how it felt to be dry.

"And there was somewhere in me the thought: By Jove! this is the deuce of an adventure – something you read about; and it is my first voyage as second mate – and I am only twenty – and here I am lasting it out as well as any of these men, and keeping my chaps up to the mark. I was pleased. I would not have given up the experience for worlds. I had moments of exultation. Whenever the old dismantled craft pitched heavily with her counter high in the air, she seemed to me to throw up, like an appeal, like a defiance, like a cry to the clouds without mercy, the words written on her stern '*Judea*, London. Do or Die.'

"O youth! The strength of it, the faith of it, the imagination of it! To me she was not an old rattle-trap carting about the world a lot of coal for a freight – to me she was the endeavour, the test, the trial of life. I think of her with pleasure, with affection, with regret – as you would think of some one dead you have loved. I shall never forget her . . . Pass the bottle.

"One night when tied to the mast, as I explained, we were pumping on, deafened with the wind, and without spirit enough in us to wish ourselves dead, a heavy sea crashed aboard and swept clean over us. As soon as I got my breath I shouted, as in duty bound, 'Keep on, boys!' when suddenly I felt something hard floating on deck strike the calf of my leg. I made a grab at it and missed. It was so dark we could not see each other's faces within a foot – you understand.

"After that thump the ship kept quiet for a while, and the thing, whatever it was, struck my leg again. This time I caught it – and it was a sauce-pan. At first, being stupid with fatigue and thinking of nothing but the pumps, I did not understand what I had in my hand. Suddenly it dawned upon me, and I shouted, 'Boys, the house on deck is gone. Leave this, and let's look for the cook.'

"There was a deck-house forward, which contained the galley, the cook's berth, and the quarters of the crew. As we had expected for days to see it swept away, the hands had been ordered to sleep in the cabin – the only safe place in the ship. The steward, Abraham, however, persisted in clinging to his berth, stupidly, like a mule – from sheer fright I believe, like an animal that won't leave a stable falling in an earthquake. So we went to look for him. It was chancing death, since once out of our lashings we were as exposed as if on a raft. But we went. The house was shattered as if a shell had exploded inside. Most of it had gone overboard – stove, men's quarters, and their property, all was gone; but two posts, holding a portion of the bulkhead to which Abraham's bunk was attached, remained as if by a miracle. We groped in the ruins and came upon this, and there he was, sitting in his bunk, surrounded by foam and wreckage, jabbering cheerfully to himself. He was out of his mind; completely and for ever mad, with this sudden shock coming upon the fag-end of his endurance. We snatched him up, lugged him aft, and pitched him

head-first down the cabin companion. You understand
there was no time to carry him down with infinite precau-
tions and wait to see how to got on. Those below would
pick him up at the bottom of the stairs all right. We
were in a hurry to go back to the pumps. That business
could not wait. A bad leak is an inhuman thing.

"One would think that the sole purpose of that fiendish
gale had been to make a lunatic of that poor devil of a
mulatto. It eased before morning, and next day the sky
cleared, and as the sea went down the leak took up.
When it came to bending a fresh set of sails the crew
demanded to put back – and really there was nothing
else to do. Boats gone, decks swept clean, cabin gutted,
men without a stitch but what they stood in, stores
spoiled, ship strained. We put her head for home, and
– would you believe it? The wind came east right in our
teeth. It blew fresh, it blew continuously. We had to beat
up every inch of the way, but she did not leak so badly,
the water keeping comparatively smooth. Two hours'
pumping in every four is no joke – but it kept her afloat
as far as Falmouth.

"The good people there live on casualties of the sea,
and no doubt were glad to see us. A hungry crowd of
shipwrights sharpened their chisels at the sight of that
carcass of a ship. And, by Jove! they had pretty pickings
off us before they were done. I fancy the owner was
already in a tight place. There were delays. Then it was
decided to take part of the cargo out and caulk her
topsides. This was done, the repairs finished, cargo
reshipped; a new crew came on board, and we went out
– for Bankok. At the end of a week we were back again.
The crew said they weren't going to Bankok – a hundred
and fifty days' passage – in a something hooker that
wanted pumping eight hours out of the twenty-four;
and the nautical papers inserted again the little paragraph: '*Judea*. Barque. Tyne to Bankok; coals; put back
to Falmouth leaky and with crew refusing duty.'

"There were more delays – more tinkering. The owner came down for a day, and said she was as right as a little fiddle. Poor old Captain Beard looked like the ghost of a Geordie skipper – through the worry and humiliation of it. Remember he was sixty, and it was his first command. Mahon said it was a foolish business, and would end badly. I loved the ship more than ever, and wanted awfully to get to Bankok. To Bankok! Magic name, blessed name. Mesopotamia wasn't a patch on it. Remember I was twenty, and it was my first second mate's billet, and the East was waiting for me.

"We went out and anchored in the outer roads with a fresh crew – the third. She leaked worse than ever. It was as if those confounded shipwrights had actually made a hole in her. This time we did not even go outside. The crew simply refused to man the windlass.

"They towed us back to the inner harbour, and we became a fixture, a feature, an institution of the place. People pointed us out to visitors as 'That 'ere barque that's going to Bankok – has been here six months – put back three times.' On holidays the small boys pulling about in boats would hail, '*Judea*, ahoy!' and if a head showed above the rail shouted, 'Where you bound to? – Bankok?' and jeered. We were only three on board. The poor old skipper mooned in the cabin. Mahon undertook the cooking, and unexpectedly developed all a Frenchman's genius for preparing nice little messes. I looked languidly after the rigging. We became citizens of Falmouth. Every shopkeeper knew us. At the barber's or tobacconist's they asked familiarly, 'Do you think you will ever get to Bankok?' Meantime the owner, the under-writers, and the charterers squabbled amongst them-selves in London, and our pay went on . . . Pass the bottle.

"It was horrid. Morally it was worse than pumping for life. It seemed as though we had been forgotten by the world, belonged to nobody, would get nowhere; it

seemed that, as if bewitched, we would have to live for
ever and ever in that inner harbour, a derision and a
byword to generations of long-shore loafers and dishonest
boatmen. I obtained three months' pay and a five days'
leave, and made a rush for London. It took me a day
to get there and pretty well another to come back – but
three months' pay went all the same. I don't know what
I did with it. I went to a music-hall, I believe, lunched,
dined, and supped in a swell place in Regent Street, and
was back to time, with nothing but a complete set of
Byron's works and a new railway rug to show for three
months' work. The boatman who pulled me off to the
ship said: 'Hallo! I thought you had left the old thing.
*She* will never get to Bankok.' 'That's all *you* know about
it,' I said, scornfully – but I didn't like that prophecy at
all.

"Suddenly a man, some kind of agent to somebody,
appeared with full powers. He had grog-blossoms all
over his face, an indomitable energy, and was a jolly soul.
We leaped into life again. A hulk came alongside, took
our cargo, and then we went into dry dock to get our
copper stripped. No wonder she leaked. The poor thing,
strained beyond endurance by the gale, had, as if in
disgust, spat out all the oakum of her lower seams. She
was recaulked, new coppered, and made as tight as a
bottle. We went back to the hulk and reshipped our
cargo.

"Then, on a fine moonlight night, all the rats left the
ship.

"We had been infested with them. They had destroyed
our sails, consumed more stores that the crew, affably
shared our beds and our dangers, and now, when the
ship was made seaworthy, concluded to clear out. I called
Mahon to enjoy the spectacle. Rat after rat appeared on
our rail, took a last look over his shoulder, and leaped
with a hollow thud into the empty hulk. We tried to
count them, but soon lost the tale. Mahon said: 'Well,

well! don't talk to me about the intelligence of rats. They ought to have left before, when we had that narrow squeak from foundering. There you have the proof how silly is the supersitition about them. They leave a good ship for an old rotten hulk, where there is nothing to eat, too, the fools! . . . I don't believe they know what is safe or what is good for them, any more than you or I.'

"And after some more talk we agreed that the wisdom of rats had been grossly overrated, being in fact no greater than that of men.

"The story of the ship was known, by this, all up the Channel from Land's End to the Forelands, and we could get no crew on the south coast. They sent us one all complete from Liverpool, and we left once more – for Bankok.

"We had fair breezes, smooth water right into the tropics, and the old *Judea* lumbered along in the sunshine. When she went eight knots everything cracked aloft, and we tied our caps to our heads; but mostly she strolled on at the rate of three miles an hour. What could you expect? She was tired – that old ship. Her youth was where mine is – where yours is – you fellows who listen to this yarn; and what friend would throw your years and your weariness in your face? We didn't grumble at her. To us aft, at least, it seemed as though we had been born in her, reared in her, had lived in her for ages, had never known any other ship. I would just as soon have abused the old village church at home for not being a cathedral.

"And for me there was also my youth to make me patient. There was all the East before me, and all life, and the thought that I had been tried in that ship and had come out pretty well. And I thought of men of old who, centuries ago, went that road in ships that sailed no better, to the land of palms, and spices, and yellow sands, and of brown nations ruled by kings more cruel

than Nero the Roman and more splendid than Solomon
the Jew. The old bark lumbered on, heavy with her age
and the burden of her cargo, while I lived the life of
youth in ignorance and hope. She lumbered on through
an interminable procession of days; and the fresh gilding
flashed back at the setting sun, seemed to cry out over
the darkening sea the words painted on her stern, '*Judea*,
London. Do or Die.'

"Then we entered the Indian Ocean and steered
northerly for Java Head. The winds were light. Weeks
slipped by. She crawled on, do or die, and people at
home began to think of posting us as overdue.

"One Saturday evening, I being off duty, the men
asked me to give them an extra bucket of water or so –
for washing clothes. As I did not wish to screw on the
fresh-water pump so late, I went forward whistling, and
with a key in my hand to unlock the forepeak scuttle,
intending to serve the water out of a spare tank we kept
there.

"The smell down below was as unexpected as it was
frightful. One would have thought hundreds of paraffin-
lamps had been flaring and smoking in that hole for
days. I was glad to get out. The man with me coughed
and said, 'Funny smell, sir.' I answered negligently, 'It's
good for the health they say,' and walked aft.

"The first thing I did was to put my head down the
square of the midship ventilator. As I lifted the lid a
visible breath, something like a thin fog, a puff of faint
haze, rose from the opening. The ascending air was hot,
and had a heavy, sooty, paraffiny smell. I gave one sniff,
and put down the lid gently. It was no use choking
myself. The cargo was on fire.

"Next day she began to smoke in earnest. You see it
was to be expected, for though the coal was of a safe
kind, that cargo had been so handled, so broken up with
handling, that it looked more like smithy coal than
anything else. Then it had been wetted – more than

once. It rained all the time we were taking it back from the hulk, and now with this long passage it got heated, and there was another case of spontaneous combustion.

"The captain called us into the cabin. He had a chart spread on the table, and looked unhappy. He said, 'The coast of West Australia is near, but I mean to proceed to our destination. It is the hurricane month too; but we will just keep her head for Bankok, and fight the fire. No more putting back anywhere, if we all get roasted. We will try first to stifle this 'ere damned combustion by want of air.'

"We tried. We battened down everything, and still she smoked. The smoke kept coming out through imperceptible crevices; it forced itself through bulkheads and covers; it oozed here and there and everywhere in slender threads, in an invisible film, in an incomprehensible manner. It made its way into the cabin, into the forecastle; it poisoned the sheltered places on the deck, it could be sniffed as high as the mainyard. It was clear that if the smoke came out the air came in. This was disheartening. This combustion refused to be stifled.

"We resolved to try water, and took the hatches off. Enormous volumes of smoke, whitish, yellowish, thick, greasy, misty, choking, ascended as high as the trucks. All hands cleared out aft. Then the poisonous cloud blew away, and we went back to work in a smoke that was no thicker now than that of an ordinary factory chimney.

"We rigged the force-pump, got the hose along, and by-and-by it burst. Well, it was as old as the ship – a prehistoric hose, and past repair. Then we pumped with the feeble head-pump, drew water with buckets and in this way managed in time to pour lots of Indian Ocean into the main hatch. The bright stream flashed in sunshine, fell into a layer of white crawling smoke, and vanished on the black surface of coal. Steam ascended mingling with the smoke. We poured salt water as into a barrel without a bottom. It was our fate to pump in that ship, to pump out of her, to pump into her; and after keeping water out of her to save ourselves from being drowned, we frantically poured water into her to save ourselves from being burnt.

"And she crawled on, do or die, in the serene weather. The sky was a miracle of purity, a miracle of azure. The sea was polished, was blue, was pellucid, was sparkling like a precious stone, extending on all sides, all round to the horizon – as if the whole terrestrial globe had been one jewel, one colossal sapphire, a single gem fashioned into a planet. And on the lustre of the great calm waters the *Judea* glided imperceptibly, enveloped in languid and unclean vapours, in a lazy cloud that drifted to leeward, light and slow: a pestiferous cloud defiling the splendour of sea and sky.

"All this time of course we saw no fire. The cargo smouldered at the bottom somewhere. Once Mahon, as we were working side by side, said to me with a queer smile: 'Now, if she only would spring a tidy leak – like that time when we first left the Channel – it would put a stopper on this fire. Wouldn't it?' I remarked irrelevantly, 'Do you remember the rats?'

"We fought the fire and sailed the ship too as carefully as though nothing had been the matter. The steward cooked and attended on us. Of the other twelve men, eight worked while four rested. Every one took his turn, captain included. There was equality, and if not exactly fraternity, then a deal of good feeling. Sometimes a man, as he dashed a bucketful of water down the hatchway, would yell out, 'Hurrah for Bankok!' and the rest laughed. But generally we were taciturn and serious – and thirsty. Oh! how thirsty! And we had to be careful with the water. Strict allowance. The ship smoked, the sun blazed . . . Pass the bottle.

"We tried everything. We even made an attempt to dig down to the fire. No good, of course. No man could remain more than a minute below. Mahon, who went first, fainted there, and the man who went to fetch him out did likewise. We lugged them out on deck. Then I leaped down to show how easily it could be done. They had learned wisdom by that time, and contented themselves by fishing for me with a chain-hook tied to a broom-handle, I believe. I did not offer to go and fetch up my shovel, which was left down below.

"Things began to look bad. We put the long-boat into the water. The second boat was ready to swing out. We had also another, a 14-foot thing, on davits aft, where it was quite safe.

"Then, behold, the smoke suddenly decreased. We redoubled our efforts to flood the bottom of the ship. In two days there was no smoke at all. Everybody was on the broad grin. This was on a Friday. On Saturday no work, but sailing the ship of course, was done. The men washed their clothes and their faces for the first time in a fortnight, and had a special dinner given them. They spoke of spontaneous combustion with contempt, and implied *they* were the boys to put out combustions. Somehow we all felt as though we each had inherited a large fortune. But a beastly smell of burning hung about the ship. Captain Beard had hollow eyes and sunken cheeks. I had never noticed so much before how twisted and bowed he was. He and Mahon prowled soberly about hatches and ventilators, sniffing. It struck me suddenly poor Mahon was a very, very old chap. As to me, I was as pleased and proud as though I had helped to win a great naval battle. O! Youth!

"The night was fine. In the morning a homeward-bound ship passed us hull down, – the first we had seen for months; but we were nearing the land at last, Java Head being about 190 miles off, and nearly due north.

"Next day it was my watch on deck from eight to twelve. At breakfast the captain observed, 'It's wonderful how that smell hangs about the cabin.' About ten, the

mate being on the poop, I stepped down on the main-
deck for a moment. The carpenter's bench stood abaft
the mainmast: I leaned against it sucking at my pipe,
and the carpenter, a young chap, came to talk to me.
He remarked, 'I think we have done very well, haven't
we?' and then I perceived with annoyance the fool was
trying to tilt the bench. I said curtly, 'Don't, Chips,' and
immediately became aware of a queer sensation, of an
absurd delusion, – I seemed somehow to be in the air.
I heard all round me like a pent-up breath released – as
if a thousand giants simultaneously had said Phoo! –
and felt a dull concussion which made my ribs ache
suddenly. No doubt about it – I was in the air, and my
body was describing a short parabola. But short as it
was, I had the time to think several thoughts in, as far
as I can remember, the following order: 'This can't be
the carpenter – What is it? – Some accident – Submar-
ine volcano? – Coals, gas! – By Jove! we are being blown
up – Everybody's dead – I am falling into the after-
hatch – I see fire in it.'

"The coal-dust suspended in the air of the hold had
glowed dull-red at the moment of the explosion. In the
twinkling of an eye, in an infinitesimal fraction of a second
since the first tilt of the bench, I was sprawling full length
on the cargo. I picked myself up and scrambled out. It
was quick like a rebound. The deck was a wilderness of
smashed timber, lying crosswise like trees in a wood after
a hurricane; an immense curtain of soiled rags waved
gently before me – it was the mainsail blown to strips. I
thought, The masts will be toppling over directly; and to
get out of the way bolted on all-fours towards the poop-
ladder. The first person I saw was Mahon, with eyes like
saucers, his mouth open, and the long white hair standing
straight on end round his head like a silver halo. He was
just about to go down when the sight of the main-deck
stirring, heaving up, and changing into splinters before
his eyes, petrified him on the top step. I stared at him in

unbelief, and he stared at me with a queer kind of shocked curiosity. I did not know that I had no hair, no eyebrows, no eyelashes, that my young moustache was burnt off, that my face was black, one cheek laid open, my nose cut, and my chin bleeding. I had lost my cap, one of my slippers, and my shirt was torn to rags. Of all this I was not aware. I was amazed to see the ship still afloat, the poop-deck whole – and, most of all, to see anybody alive. Also the peace of the sky and the serenity of the sea were distinctly surprising. I suppose I expected to see them convulsed with horror . . . Pass the bottle.

"There was a voice hailing the ship from somewhere – in the air, in the sky – I couldn't tell. Presently I saw the captain – and he was mad. He asked me eagerly, 'Where's the cabin-table?' and to hear such a question was a frightful shock. I had just been blown up, you understand, and vibrated with that experience, – I wasn't quite sure whether I was alive. Mahon began to stamp with both feet and yelled at him, 'Good God! don't you see the deck's blown out of her?' I found my voice, and stammered out as if conscious of some gross neglect of duty, 'I don't know where the cabin-table is.' It was like an absurd dream.

"Do you know what he wanted next? Well, he wanted to trim the yards. Very placidly, and as if lost in thought, he insisted on having the foreyard squared. 'I don't know if there's anybody alive,' said Mahon, almost tearfully. 'Surely,' he said, gently, 'there will be enough left to square the foreyard.'

"The old chap, it seems, was in his own berth, winding up the chronometers, when the shock sent him spinning. Immediately it occurred to him – as he said afterwards – that the ship had struck something, and he ran out into the cabin. There, he saw, the cabin-table had vanished somewhere. The deck being blown up, it had fallen down into the lazarette of course. Where we had our breakfast that morning he saw only a great hole in the floor. This appeared to him so awfully mysterious, and impressed him so immensely, that what he saw and heard after he got on deck were mere trifles in comparison. And, mark, he noticed directly the wheel deserted and his barque off her course – and his only thought was to get that miserable, stripped, undecked, smouldering shell of a ship back again with her head pointing at her port of destination. Bankok! That's what he was after. I tell you this quiet, bowed, bandy-legged, almost deformed little man was immense in the singleness of his idea and in his placid ignorance of our agitation. He motioned us forward with a commanding gesture, and went to take the wheel himself.

"Yes; that was the first thing we did – trim the yards of that wreck! No one was killed, or even disabled, but every one was more or less hurt. You should have seen them! Some were in rags, with black faces, like coalheavers, like sweeps, and had bullet heads that seemed closely cropped, but were in fact singed to the skin. Others, of the watch below, awakened by being shot out from their collapsing bunks, shivered incessantly, and kept on groaning even as we went about our work. But they all worked. That crew of Liverpool hard cases had in them the right stuff. It's my experience they always have. It is the sea that gives it – the vastness, the loneliness surrounding their dark stolid souls. Ah! Well! we stumbled, we crept, we fell, we barked our shins on the wreckage, we hauled. The masts stood, but we did not know how much they might be charred down below. It was nearly calm, but a long swell ran from the west and made her roll. They might go at any moment. We looked at them with apprehension. One could not foresee which way they would fall.

"Then we retreated aft and looked about us. The deck was a tangle of planks on edge, of planks on end, of splinters, of ruined woodwork. The masts rose from that chaos like big trees above a matted undergrowth. The interstices of that mass of wreckage were full of something whitish, sluggish, stirring – of something that was like a greasy fog. The smoke of the invisible fire was coming up again, was trailing, like a poisonous thick mist in some valley choked with dead wood. Already lazy wisps were beginning to curl upwards amongst the mass of splinters. Here and there a piece of timber, stuck upright, resembled a post. Half of a fife-rail had been shot through the foresail, and the sky made a patch of glorious blue in the ignobly soiled canvas. A portion of several boards holding together had fallen across the rail, and one end protruded overboard, like a gangway leading upon nothing, like a gangway leading over the deep sea, leading to death – as if inviting us to walk the plank at once and be done with our ridiculous troubles. And still the air, the sky – a ghost, something invisible was hailing the ship.

"Some one had the sense to look over, and there was the helmsman, who had impulsively jumped overboard, anxious to come back. He yelled and swam lustily like a merman, keeping up with the ship. We threw him a rope, and presently he stood amongst us streaming with water and very crestfallen. The captain had surrendered the wheel, and apart, elbow on rail and chin in hand, gazed at the sea wistfully. We asked ourselves, What next? I thought, Now, this is something like. This is great. I wonder what will happen. O youth!

"Suddenly Mahon sighted a steamer far astern. Captain Beard said, 'We may do something with her yet.' We hoisted two flags, which said in the international language of the sea, 'On fire. Want immediate assistance.' The steamer grew bigger rapidly, and by-and-by spoke with two flags on her foremast, 'I am coming to your assistance.'

"In half an hour she was abreast, to windward, within hail, and rolling slightly, with her engines stopped. We lost our composure, and yelled all together with excitement, 'We've been blown up.' A man in a white helmet, on the bridge, cried, 'Yes! All right! All right!' and he nodded his head, and smiled, and made soothing motions with his hand as though at a lot of frightened children. One of the boats dropped in the water, and walked towards us upon the sea with her long oars. Four Calashes pulled a swinging stroke. This was my first sight of Malay seamen. I've known them since, but what struck me then was their unconcern: they came alongside, and even the bowman standing up and holding to our main-chains with the boat-hook did not deign to lift his head for a glance. I thought people who had been blown up deserved more attention.

"A little man, dry like a chip and agile like a monkey, clambered up. It was the mate of the steamer. He gave one look, and cried, 'O boys – you had better quit.'

"We were silent. He talked apart with the captain for a time, – seemed to argue with him. Then they went away together to the steamer.

"When our skipper came back we learned that the steamer was the *Sommerville*, Captain Nash, from West Australia to Singapore *viâ* Batavia with mails, and that the agreement was she should tow us to Anjer or Batavia, if possible, where we could extinguish the fire by scuttling, and then proceed on our voyage – to Bankok! The old man seemed excited. 'We will do it yet,' he said to Mahon, fiercely. He shook his fist at the sky. Nobody else said a word.

"At noon the steamer began to tow. She went ahead slim and high, and what was left of the *Judea* followed at the end of seventy fathom of tow-rope, – followed her swiftly like a cloud of smoke with mastheads protruding above. We went aloft to furl the sails. We coughed on the yards, and were careful about the bunts. Do you see the lot of us there, putting a neat furl on the sails of that ship doomed to arrive nowhere? There was not a man who didn't think that at any moment

the masts would topple over. From aloft we could not
see the ship for smoke, and they worked carefully, passing
the gaskets with even turns. 'Harbour furl – aloft there!'
cried Mahon from below.

"You understand this? I don't think one of those chaps
expected to get down in the usual way. When we did I
heard them saying to each other, 'Well, I thought we
would come down overboard, in a lump – sticks and all
– blame me if I didn't.' 'That's what I was thinking to
myself,' would answer wearily another battered and band-
aged scarecrow. And, mind, these were men without the
drilled-in habit of obedience. To an onlooker they would
be a lot of profane scallywags without a redeeming point.
What made them do it – what made them obey me
when I, thinking consciously how fine it was, made
them drop the bunt of the foresail twice to try and do
it better? What? They had no professional reputation –
no examples, no praise. It wasn't a sense of duty; they
all knew well enough how to shirk, and laze, and dodge
– when they had a mind to it – and mostly they had.
Was it the two pounds ten a-month that sent them
there? They didn't think their pay half good enough.
No; it was something in them, something inborn and
subtle and everlasting. I don't say positively that the crew
of a French or German merchantman wouldn't have done
it, but I doubt whether it would have been done in the
same way. There was a completeness in it, something
solid like a principle, and masterful like an instinct – a
disclosure of something secret – of that hidden something, that gift of good or evil that makes racial difference, that shapes the fate of nations.

"It was that night at ten that, for the first time since
we had been fighting it, we saw the fire. The speed of
the towing had fanned the smouldering destruction. A
blue gleam appeared forward, shining below the wreck
of the deck. It wavered in patches, it seemed to stir and
creep like the light of a glowworm. I saw it first, and

told Mahon. 'Then the game's up,' he said. 'We had better stop this towing, or she will burst out suddenly fore and aft before we can clear out.' We set up a yell; rang bells to attract their attention; they towed on. At last Mahon and I had to crawl forward and cut the rope with an axe. There was no time to cast off the lashings. Red tongues could be seen licking the wilderness of splinters under our feet as we made our way back to the poop.

"Of course they very soon found out in the steamer that the rope was gone. She gave a loud blast of her whistle, her lights were seen sweeping in a wide circle, she came up ranging close alongside, and stopped. We were all in a tight group on the poop looking at her. Every man had saved a little bundle or a bag. Suddenly a conical flame with a twisted top shot up forward and threw upon the black sea a circle of light, with the two vessels side by side and heaving gently in its centre. Captain Beard had been sitting on the gratings still and mute for hours, but now he rose slowly and advanced in front of us, to the mizzen-shrouds. Captain Nash hailed: 'Come along! Look sharp. I have mail-bags on board. I will take you and your boats to Singapore.'

"'Thank you! No!' said our skipper. 'We must see the last of the ship.'

"'I can't stand by any longer,' shouted the other. 'Mails – you know.'

"'Ay! ay! We are all right.'

"'Very well! I'll report you in Singapore . . . Good-bye!'

"He waved his hand. Our men dropped their bundles quietly. The steamer moved ahead, and passing out of the circle of light, vanished at once from our sight, dazzled by the fire which burned fiercely. And then I knew that I would see the East first as commander of a small boat. I thought it fine; and the fidelity to the old ship was fine. We should see the last of her. Oh the glamour of youth! Oh the fire of it, more dazzling than the flames of the burning ship, throwing a magic light on the wide earth, leaping audaciously to the sky, presently to be quenched by time, more cruel, more pitiless, more bitter than the sea – and like the flames of the burning ship surrounded by an impenetrable night.

"The old man warned us in his gentle and inflexible way that it was part of our duty to save for the underwriters as much as we could of the ship's gear. Accordingly we went to work aft, while she blazed forward to give us plenty of light. We lugged out a lot of rubbish. What didn't we save? An old barometer fixed with an absurd quantity of screws nearly cost me my life: a sudden rush of smoke came upon me, and I just got away in time. There were various stores, bolts of canvas, coils of rope; the poop looked like a marine bazaar, and the boats were lumbered to the gunwales. One would have thought the old man wanted to take as much as he could of his first command with him. He was very, very quiet, but off his balance evidently. Would you believe it? He wanted to take a length of old stream-cable and a kedge-anchor with him in the long-boat. We said, 'Ay, ay, sir,' deferentially, and on the quiet let the things slip overboard. The heavy medicine-chest went that way, two bags of green coffee, tins of paint – fancy, paint! – a whole lot of things. Then I was ordered with two hands into the boats to make a stowage and get them ready against the time it would be proper for us to leave the ship.

"We put everything straight, stepped the long-boat's mast for our skipper, who was to take charge of her, and I was not sorry to sit down for a moment. My face felt raw, every limb ached as if broken, I was aware of all my ribs, and would have sworn to a twist in the backbone. The boats, fast astern, lay in a deep shadow, and all around I could see the circle of the sea lighted by

the fire. A gigantic flame rose forward straight and clear.
It flared fierce, with noises like the whirr of wings, with
rumbles as of thunder. There were cracks, detonations,
and from the cone of flame the sparks flew upwards, as
man is born to trouble, to leaky ships, and to ships that
burn.

"What bothered me was that the ship, lying broadside to the swell and to such wind as there was – a mere
breath – the boats would not keep astern where they
were safe, but persisted, in a pig-headed way boats have,
in getting under the counter and then swinging alongside. They were knocking about dangerously and coming
near the flame, while the ship rolled on them, and, of
course, there was always the danger of the masts going
over the side at any moment. I and my two boat-keepers
kept them off as best we could, with oars and boat-
hooks; but to be constantly at it became exasperating,
since there was no reason why we should not leave at
once. We could not see those on board, nor could we
imagine what caused the delay. The boat-keepers were
swearing feebly, and I had not only my share of the work
but also had to keep at it two men who showed a constant
inclination to lay themselves down and let things slide.

"At last I hailed, 'On deck there,' and some one looked
over. 'We're ready here,' I said. The head disappeared,
and very soon popped up again. 'The captain says, All
right, sir, and to keep the boats well clear of the ship.'

"Half an hour passed. Suddenly there was a frightful
racket, rattle, clanking of chain, hiss of water, and millions
of sparks flew up into the shivering column of smoke
that stood leaning slightly above the ship. The cat-heads
had burned away, and the two red-hot anchors had gone
to the bottom, tearing out after them two hundred fathom
of red-hot chain. The ship trembled, the mass of flame
swayed as if ready to collapse, and the fore top-gallant-
mast fell. It darted down like an arrow of fire, shot under,
and instantly leaping up within an oar's-length of the

boats, floated quietly, very black on the luminous sea. I
hailed the deck again. After some time a man in an
unexpectedly cheerful but also muffled tone, as though
he had been trying to speak with his mouth shut,
informed me, 'Coming directly, sir,' and vanished. For a
long time I heard nothing but the whirr and roar of the
fire. There were also whistling sounds. The boats jumped,
tugged at the painters, ran at each other playfully, knocked
their sides together, or, do what we would, swung in a
bunch against the ship's side. I couldn't stand it any
longer, and swarming up a rope, clambered aboard over
the stern.

"It was as bright as day. Coming up like this, the sheet
of fire facing me, was a terrifying sight, and the heat
seemed hardly bearable at first. On a settee cushion
dragged out of the cabin, Captain Beard, his legs drawn
up and one arm under his head, slept with the light
playing on him. Do you know what the rest were busy
about? They were sitting on deck right aft, round an
open case, eating bread and cheese and drinking bottled
stout.

"On the background of flames twisting in fierce
tongues above their heads they seemed at home like
salamanders, and looked like a band of desperate pirates.
The fire sparkled in the whites of their eyes, gleamed
on patches of white skin seen through the torn shirts.
Each had the marks as of a battle about him – ban-
daged heads, tied-up arms, a strip of dirty rag round a
knee – and each man had a bottle between his legs and
a chunk of cheese in his hand. Mahon got up. With his
handsome and disreputable head, his hooked profile,
his long white beard, and with an uncorked bottle in
his hand, he resembled one of those reckless sea-robbers
of old making merry amidst violence and disaster. 'The
last meal on board,' he explained solemnly. 'We had
nothing to eat all day, and it was no use leaving all this.'
He flourished the bottle and indicated the sleeping

skipper. 'He said he couldn't swallow anything, so I got him to lie down,' he went on; and as I stared, 'I don't know whether you are aware, young fellow, the man had no sleep to speak of for days – and there will be dam' little sleep in the boats.' 'There will be no boats by-and-by if you fool about much longer,' I said, indignantly. I walked up to the skipper and shook him by the shoulder. At last he opened his eyes, but did not move. 'Time to leave her, sir,' I said, quietly.

"He got up painfully, looked at the flames, at the sea sparkling round the ship, and black, black as ink farther away; he looked at the stars shining dim through a thin veil of smoke in a sky black, black as Erebus.

"'Youngest first,' he said.

"And the ordinary seaman, wiping his mouth with the back of his hand, got up, clambered over the taffrail, and vanished. Others followed. One, on the point of going over, stopped short to drain his bottle, and with a great swing of his arm flung it at the fire. 'Take this!' he cried.

"The skipper lingered disconsolately, and we left him to commune alone for a while with his first command. Then I went up again and brought him away at last. It was time. The ironwork on the poop was hot to the touch.

"Then the painter of the long-boat was cut, and the three boats, tied together, drifted clear of the ship. It was just sixteen hours after the explosion when we abandoned her. Mahon had charge of the second boat, and I had the smallest – the 14-foot thing. The long-boat would have taken the lot of us; but the skipper said we must save as much property as we could – for the underwriters – and so I got my first command. I had two men with me, a bag of biscuits, a few tins of meat, and a breaker of water. I was ordered to keep close to the long-boat, that in case of bad weather we might be taken into her.

"And do you know what I thought? I thought I would part company as soon as I could. I wanted to have my first command all to myself. I wasn't going to sail in a squadron if there were a chance for independent cruising. I would make land by myself. I would beat the other boats. Youth! All youth! The silly, charming, beautiful youth.

"But we did not make a start at once. We must see the last of the ship. And so the boats drifted about that night, heaving and setting on the swell. The men dozed, waked, sighed, groaned. I looked at the burning ship.

"Between the darkness of earth and heaven she was burning fiercely upon a disc of purple sea shot by the blood-red play of gleams; upon a disc of water glittering and sinister. A high, clear flame, an immense and lonely flame, ascended from the ocean, and from its summit the black smoke poured continously at the sky. She burned furiously, mournful and imposing like a funeral pile kindled in the night, surrounded by the sea, watched over by the stars. A magnificent death had come like a grace, like a gift, like a reward to that old ship at the end of her laborious days. The surrender of her weary ghost to the keeping of stars and sea was stirring like the sight of a glorious triumph. The masts fell just before daybreak, and for a moment there was a burst and turmoil of sparks that seemed to fill with flying fire the night patient and watchful, the vast night lying silent upon the sea. At daylight she was only a charred shell, floating still under a cloud of smoke and bearing a glowing mass of coal within.

"Then the oars were got out, and the boats forming in a line moved round her remains as if in procession – the long-boat leading. As we pulled across her stern a slim dart of fire shot out viciously at us, and suddenly she went down, head first, in a great hiss of steam. The unconsumed stern was the last to sink; but the paint had gone, had cracked, had peeled off, and there were no letters, there was no word, no stubborn device that was like her soul, to flash at the rising sun her creed and her name.

"We made our way north. A breeze sprang up, and about noon all the boats came together for the last time. I had no mast or sail in mine, but I made a mast out of a spare oar and hoisted a boat-awning for a sail, with a boat-hook for a yard. She was certainly over-masted, but I had the satisfaction of knowing that with the wind aft I could beat the other two. I had to wait for them. Then we all had a look at the captain's chart, and, after a sociable meal of hard bread and water, got our last instructions. These were simple: steer north, and keep together as much as possible. 'Be careful with that jury-rig, Marlow,' said the captain; and Mahon, as I sailed proudly past his boat, wrinkled his curved nose and hailed, 'You will sail that ship of yours under water, if you don't look out, young fellow.' He was a malicious old man – and may the deep sea where he sleeps now rock him gently, rock him tenderly to the end of time!

"Before sunset a thick rain-squall passed over the two boats, which were far astern, and that was the last I saw of them for a time. Next day I sat steering my cockle-shell – my first command – with nothing but water and sky around me. I did sight in the afternoon the upper sails of a ship far away, but said nothing, and my men did not notice her. You see I was afraid she might be homeward bound, and I had no mind to turn back from the portals of the East. I was steering for Java – another blessed name – like Bankok, you know. I steered many days.

"I need not tell you what it is to be knocking about in an open boat. I remember nights and days of calm when we pulled, we pulled, and the boat seemed to stand still, as if bewitched within the circle of the sea horizon. I remember the heat, the deluge of rain-squalls that kept us baling for dear life (but filled our water-cask), and I

remember sixteen hours on end with a mouth dry as a
cinder and a steering-oar over the stern to keep my first
command head on to a breaking sea. I did not know
how good a man I was till then. I remember the drawn
faces, the dejected figures of my two men, and I remember
my youth and the feeling that will never come back any
more – the feeling that I could last for ever, outlast the
sea, the earth, and all men; the deceitful feeling that
lures us on to joys, to perils, to love, to vain effort – to
death; the triumphant conviction of strength, the heat
of life in the handful of dust, the glow in the heart that
with every year grows dim, grows cold, grows small, and
expires – and expires, too soon, too soon – before life
itself.

"And this is how I see the East. I have seen its secret
places and have looked into its very soul; but now I see
it always from a small boat, a high outline of moun-
tains, blue and afar in the morning; like faint mist at
noon; a jagged wall of purple at sunset. I have the feel
of the oar in my hand, the vision of a scorching blue
sea in my eyes. And I see a bay, a wide bay, smooth as
glass and polished like ice, shimmering in the dark. A
red light burns far off upon the gloom of the land, and
the night is soft and warm. We drag at the oars with
aching arms, and suddenly a puff of wind, a puff faint
and tepid and laden with strange odours of blossoms,
of aromatic wood, comes out of the still night – the first
sigh of the East on my face. That I can never forget. It
was impalpable and enslaving, like a charm, like a whispered promise of mysterious delight.

"We had been pulling this finishing spell for eleven
hours. Two pulled, and he whose turn it was to rest sat
at the tiller. We had made out the red light in that bay
and steered for it, guessing it must mark some small
coasting port. We passed two vessels, outlandish and
high-sterned, sleeping at anchor, and, approaching the
light, now very dim, ran the boat's nose against the end

of a jutting wharf. We were blind with fatigue. My men dropped the oars and fell off the thwarts as if dead. I made fast to a pile. A current rippled softly. The scented obscurity of the shore was grouped into vast masses, a density of colossal clumps of vegetation, probably – mute and fantastic shapes. And at their foot the semi-circle of a beach gleamed faintly, like an illusion. There was not a light, not a stir, not a sound. The mysterious East faced me, perfumed like a flower, silent like death, dark like a grave.

"And I sat weary beyond expression, exulting like a conqueror, sleepless and entranced as if before a profound, a fateful enigma.

"A splashing of oars, a measured dip reverberating on the level of water, intensified by the silence of the shore into loud claps, made me jump up. A boat, a European boat, was coming in. I invoked the name of the dead; I hailed: *Judea* ahoy! A thin shout answered.

"It was the captain. I had beaten the flagship by three hours, and I was glad to hear the old man's voice again, tremulous and tired. 'Is it you, Marlow?' 'Mind the end of that jetty, sir,' I cried.

"He approached cautiously, and brought up with the deep-sea lead-line which we had saved – for the under-writers. I eased my painter and fell alongside. He sat, a broken figure at the stern, wet with dew, his hands clasped in his lap. His men were asleep already. 'I had a terrible time of it,' he murmured. Mahon is behind – not very far.' We conversed in whispers, in low whispers, as if afraid to wake up the land. Guns, thunder, earthquakes would not have awakened the men just then.

"Looking round as we talked, I saw away at sea a bright light travelling in the night. 'There's a steamer passing the bay,' I said. She was not passing, she was entering, and she even came close and anchored. 'I wish,' said the old man, 'you would find out whether she is English. Perhaps they could give us a passage somewhere.'

He seemed nervously anxious. So by dint of punching and kicking I started one of my men into a state of somnambulism, and giving him an oar, took another and pulled towards the lights of the steamer.

"There was a murmur of voices in her, metallic hollow clangs of the engine-room, footsteps on the deck. Her ports shone, round like dilated eyes. Shapes moved about, and there was a shadowy man high up on the bridge. He heard my oars.

"And then, before I could open my lips, the East spoke to me, but it was in a Western voice. A torrent of words was poured into the enigmatical, the fateful silence; outlandish, angry words, mixed with words and even whole sentences of good English, less strange but even more surprising. The voice swore and cursed violently; it riddled the solemn peace of the bay by a volley of abuse. It began by calling me Pig, and from that went crescendo into unmentionable adjectives – in English. The man up there raged aloud in two languages, and with a sincerity in his fury that almost convinced me I had, in some way, sinned against the harmony of the universe. I could hardly see him, but began to think he would work himself into a fit.

"Suddenly he ceased, and I could hear him snorting and blowing like a porpoise. I said –

"'What steamer is this, pray?'

"'Eh? What's this? And who are you?'

"'Castaway crew of an English barque burnt at sea. We came here to-night. I am the second mate. The captain is in the long-boat, and wishes to know if you would give us a passage somewhere.'

"'Oh, my goodness! I say . . . This is the *Celestial* from Singapore on her return trip. I'll arrange with your captain in the morning, . . . and, . . . I say, . . . did you hear me just now?'

"'I should think the whole bay heard you.'

"'I thought you were a shore-boat. Now, look here –

this infernal lazy scoundrel of a caretaker has gone to sleep again – curse him. The light is out, and I nearly ran foul of the end of this damned jetty. This is the third time he plays me this trick. Now, I ask you, can anybody stand this kind of thing? It's enough to drive a man out of his mind. I'll report him . . . I'll get the Assistant Resident to give him the sack, by . . . ! See – there's no light. It's out, isn't it? I take you to witness the light's out. There should be a light, you know. A red light on the—'

"'There was a light,' I said, mildly.

"'But it's out, man! What's the use of talking like this? You can see for yourself it's out – don't you? If you had to take a valuable steamer along this God-forsaken coast you would want a light too. I'll kick him from end to end of his miserable wharf. You'll see if I don't. I will—'

"'So I may tell my captain you'll take us?' I broke in.

"'Yes, I'll take you. Good night,' he said, brusquely.

"I pulled back, made fast again to the jetty, and then went to sleep at last. I had faced the silence of the East. I had heard some of its language. But when I opened my eyes again the silence was as complete as though it had never been broken. I was lying in a flood of light, and the sky had never looked so far, so high, before. I opened my eyes and lay without moving.

"And then I saw the men of the East – they were looking at me. The whole length of the jetty was full of people. I saw brown, bronze, yellow faces, the black eyes, the glitter, the colour of an Eastern crowd. And all these beings stared without a murmur, without a sigh, without a movement. They stared down at the boats, at the sleeping men who at night had come to them from the sea. Nothing moved. The fronds of palms stood still against the sky. Not a branch stirred along the shore, and the brown roofs of hidden houses peeped through the green foliage, through the big leaves that hung shining and still like leaves forged of heavy metal. This was the East of the ancient navigators, so old, so mysterious, resplendent and sombre, living and unchanged, full of danger and promise. And these were the men. I sat up suddenly. A wave of movement passed through the crowd from end to end, passed along the heads, swayed the bodies, ran along the jetty like a ripple on the water, like a breath of wind on a field – and all was still again. I see it now – the wide sweep of the bay, the glittering sands, the wealth of green infinite and varied, the sea blue like the sea of a dream, the crowd of attentive faces, the blaze of vivid colour – the water reflecting it all, the curve of the shore, the jetty, the high-sterned outlandish craft floating still, and the three boats with the tired men from the West sleeping, unconscious of the land and the people and of the violence of sunshine. They slept thrown across the thwarts, curled on bottom-boards, in the careless attitudes of death. The head of the old skipper, leaning back in the stern of the long-boat, had fallen on his breast, and he looked as though he would never wake. Farther out old Mahon's face was upturned to the sky, with the long white beard spread out on his breast, as though he had been shot where he sat at the tiller; and a man, all in a heap in the bows of the boat, slept with both arms embracing the stem-head and with his cheek laid on the gunwale. The East looked at them without a sound.

"I have known its fascination since: I have seen the mysterious shores, the still water, the lands of brown nations, where a stealthy Nemesis lies in wait, pursues, overtakes so many of the conquering race, who are proud of their wisdom, of their knowledge, of their strength. But for me all the East is contained in that vision of my youth. It is all in that moment when I opened my young eyes on it. I came upon it from a tussle with the sea – and I was young – and I saw it looking at me. And this is all that is left of it! Only a

moment; a moment of strength, of romance, of glamour
– of youth! . . . A flick of sunshine upon a strange
shore, the time to remember, the time for a sigh, and
– good-bye! – Night – Good-bye . . . !"

He drank.

"Ah! The good old time – the good old time. Youth
and the sea. Glamour and the sea! The good, strong sea,
the salt, bitter sea, that could whisper to you and roar
at you and knock your breath out of you."

He drank again.

"By all that's wonderful, it is the sea, I believe, the
sea itself – or is it youth alone? Who can tell? But you
here – you all had something out of life: money, love –
whatever one gets on shore – and, tell me, wasn't that
the best time, that time when we were young at sea;
young and had nothing, on the sea that gives nothing,
except hard knocks – and sometimes a chance to feel
your strength – that only – what you all regret?"

And we all nodded at him: the man of finance, the
man of accounts, the man of law, we all nodded at him
over the polished table that like a still sheet of brown
water reflected our faces, lined, wrinkled; our faces
marked by toil, by deceptions, by success, by love; our
weary eyes looking still, looking always, looking
anxiously for something out of life, that while it is
expected is already gone – has passed unseen, in a sigh,
in a flash – together with the youth, with the strength,
with the romance of illusions.

# THE HISTORY OF VINTAGE

The famous American publisher Alfred A. Knopf (1892–1984) founded Vintage Books in the United States in 1954 as a paperback home for the authors published by his company. Vintage was launched in the United Kingdom in 1990 and works independently from the American imprint although both are part of the international publishing group, Random House.

Vintage in the United Kingdom was initially created to publish paperback editions of books acquired by the prestigious hardback imprints in the Random House Group such as Jonathan Cape, Chatto & Windus, Hutchinson and later William Heinemann, Secker & Warburg and The Harvill Press. There are many Booker and Nobel Prize-winning authors on the Vintage list and the imprint publishes a huge variety of fiction and non-fiction. Over the years Vintage has expanded and the list now includes both great authors of the past – who are published under the Vintage Classics imprint – as well as many of the most influential authors of the present.

For a full list of the books Vintage publishes, please visit our website
www.vintage-books.co.uk

For book details and other information about the classic authors we publish, please visit the Vintage Classics website
www.vintage-classics.info

www.vintage-classics.info